Teen

Dedicated

To Sarah and Nat,

Sisters from other misters

Teen Superheroes

Book Five

Terminal Fear

Prolog

My name's Axel and I'm a teenage superhero.

I know that sounds crazy, but it's the truth. I'm one of five teenagers who had their memories wiped and were given incredible powers by a secret organization known as The Agency. Now we're on the run from them, and if we're caught, we'll end up in jail—or worse.

My name is Axel, but it could be anything. We were given names corresponding to the first five letters of the alphabet. I can control air, turn it into weapons, create barriers or fly on it.

B stands for Brodie. She's a red-haired Australian girl, with the strength and agility of three grown men. You wouldn't want to be in a fight with her. You might win, but it's unlikely. She was my girlfriend until recently, but all that changed because of Chad.

Which brings me to the letter C. Chad is a Norwegian who can control fire and ice. Oh, and he's a complete pain. He's also my friend, but our friendship was tested in our last adventure when we saw a future where he and Brodie were a couple. Mind you, we've changed that future, but history might repeat itself. That possibility is never far from my mind.

Now you're probably wondering what D stands for. Well, it's Dan. He's the youngest of us, probably fourteen. He's Chinese, but speaks perfect English and can control metal from a distance. Dan can also read and manipulate minds, but those powers don't work all the time, so he doesn't use them much. Unreliable powers can get you killed.

Then there's Ebony. She's Chad's sister and completely unlike him. Quieter and easygoing, there's a tiger beneath her shy exterior. Able to change one substance into another, she can turn a wall into air, or transform granite to lead. It's a good talent to have. Turning iron into gold is handy, too, when you need money—and we always do.

And now, I come to the final member of our team—Ferdy. He started off like the rest of us. Sort of. Suffering from autism, he recently had his consciousness converted to energy. It should have been a death sentence, but he somehow survived the whole experience and he now lives in the computer of our spaceship, *Liber8tor*.

In a way, *Liber8tor* has become a member of our crew. Once owned by a race of beings known as the Tagaar, it has become our home, and it allows us to travel anywhere around the globe. Without *Liber8tor*, The Agency would have caught up with us long ago.

The world has changed a lot in the last few months. There are superheroes in every country and The Agency has branches everywhere. There's also a town—New Haven—in the state of Virginia where the occupants of a recently crashed spacecraft now live.

And that's about it. We're trying to discover our true identities while staying one step ahead of the law. It's not an easy life, but it's the only one we've got. We don't know what tomorrow will bring.

Who does?

Chapter One

'Felix?' Mavis Shaw said. 'Is that you?'

If Felix had answered with anything other than a meow, she would have been amazed. Felix was her seven year old cat—an American shorthair—and had taken to wandering late in the day. Now it was 5pm and there was no sign of her.

Mavis sighed. She was seventy-seven years old and although she would never run another marathon, her health was generally good. Privately, she hoped to see another dozen summers before her mind went. Her husband, Harry, spared the indignity of dementia, had been taken quietly in his sleep two years ago.

Her two sons had moved away from the little town of Targo, leaving her alone, but she wasn't lonely. She had lived here all her life, and was known and respected. Maybe that didn't mean much in a lot of communities, but it did in Targo. It was a *good* town. A nice place to raise kids, grow old and, yes, even a good place to die when the time came.

It's My Life was about to start on television,

and she would miss the beginning if she went cat hunting. Groaning, she threw on a coat. Mavis didn't relish problems, but life had a way of dishing them out, anyway.

You'd think I'd be used to trouble, she thought.

Her screen door squealed open as she peered out at the same vista she had seen for the last half a century. Hers was the second last house in the street, the final one being the old Cooper place. Beyond it was miles of forest.

Felix was nowhere to be seen among the potted plants that crowded her veranda. Nor was she lurking under the rose bushes in her busy front garden.

Across the road, it was quiet. *Dead* quiet, those with a sense of humor would say, because it was the Targo town cemetery. Lord knows she and Harry had told, and retold, every bad joke about the place over their fifty year marriage.

Everyone's dying to go there.

You need a skeleton key to get out.

A guy over there's looking for his ghoul friend. Get it? Ghoul friend...

Ha ha. Or as the young folks would say, LOL. Whatever that meant.

Darkness fell early, here in the mountains. There was no reason to suspect anything had happened to Felix. Maybe she'd just gone wandering, searching for a boyfriend. The Smiths, who had just moved in down the hill, had a cat. An Abyssinian. Maybe Felix was on a date.

Skeeeeeellllll.

The sound was barely recognizable as a scream. It wasn't human. But it did sound horribly, vaguely, feline.

Felix.

Mavis peered up and down the street. The Smiths were half a mile down the hill. There was no movement at their place, and they didn't arrive home till late anyway. They both worked in town—Bert at the library, and Sarah at a legal firm. There wasn't anything at their place that could hurt Felix anyway. Cats weren't stupid creatures and Felix wasn't an exception.

Her eyes strayed to the old Cooper House. It *was* an old building. Not derelict by any means, but nobody had lived there for twenty years. It belonged to her and Harry, or her, now that Harry was gone. As investments went, it was a stinker. They had never been able to rent it out because of the house's history. Their accountant had urged them to sell it a dozen times over the years, but they had hung onto it for the land value.

The building even scared her. Targo cemetery wasn't haunted, but the old Cooper place was a different matter...

Felix wouldn't have wandered up there, she thought. *That old cat would have no reason to...*

The scream rang out again.

Choking back a cry, Mavis charged up the road, but not before snatching up the rake from her front yard. Maybe that fool cat had gotten herself into trouble, or maybe somebody had brought trouble to it, but either way she wasn't losing her cat. Not so soon after Harry.

She had seen someone near the house recently. Joey Kent. He was a bad boy, all right, his father in jail, and his mother an alcoholic. Bad kids were always looking for mischief, and they all too easily found it.

Reaching the front gate, Mavis paused. The house was an old gothic building, the paint peeling, the roof missing tiles and the iron fence red with rust. Chickweed, kudzu and ground ivy choked the grounds. Buried under that jungle were rose bushes and cheerless garden gnomes.

Pushing the front gate open was like hearing something in pain. Making her way up the cracked front path, Mavis suddenly noticed how hard her heart was beating.

Mavis Shaw, she thought. *You're a tough old bird. Haunted houses don't scare you. Or delinquent children.*

And she had her rake for protection. A poke to the eye or a jab between the legs would bring down any assailant. And Joey Kent might be bad, but she could handle him.

So why was she so terrified?

As always, the front door was closed and locked. So were the windows. All looked fine. She squinted through dusty glass. The room beyond looked identical to how she remembered it; a few pieces of furniture with throwover sheets to keep them protected.

We should have burnt this place down years ago, Mavis thought. *And collected the insurance.*

But she and Harry didn't operate that way.

The sound came again, louder this time, and obviously from the rear. Tightening her grip on the rake, she rounded the building, trampling through undergrowth. Night was near. The sun had disappeared behind the mountains and insects were starting to chirrup in the undergrowth.

Mavis shivered, as much from the cold as the fear jangling her nerves. The back yard was silent and deserted, the rear porch drowned in shadow.

Cautiously climbing the stairs, Mavis glanced through the back window, but it was too dark to make out anything.

'Felix?' she called. 'Here, Felix.'

A tiny squeak came from inside. Felix must be in the building. But how? Maybe that brat, Joey Kent, had locked her in. Gripping the door handle, she gave it a twist and shoved it open.

'Felix?'

No answer. Even the buzz of the insects had faded. It was so quiet, Mavis could almost hear her own heart beating. A vein throbbed uncomfortably in her throat.

'Joey Kent,' she said. 'There'll be hell to pay if you've hurt my cat.'

Shaking the rake threateningly, Mavis stepped into the room. At first, she could see nothing. Just more furniture shrouded in sheets and gloomy shadows. Then one of the shadows moved.

Mavis gasped. Feeling light-headed, she grasped the doorframe as a man stepped from the dark. He looked like something from a nightmare. Wearing a long coat, buttoned to the neck, the only visible skin was scarred, as if he had survived a terrible fire. His hair had been reduced to a few clumps, and his eyes seemed to poke out from his face like two perfectly white golf balls. The fire had taken his lips too, reducing his face to a grinning skull.

'Who...' Mavis struggled to speak. 'Who are you?'

The man strolled across the room until his face was only inches from her own. His breathe was all too human; it smelt of onions.

'Who I am is not important,' he said. 'But I would advise you to think of something pleasant.'

'Why?' Her terrified voice was like a squeak. 'What are you saying?'

She tried lifting the rake, but the scarred man already had an object in his hand. The size of a pen, the end glowed cornflower blue.

'You should think nice thoughts at the end,' he said.

That was the last thing Mavis heard. Her vision went dark, and she was only dimly aware of the rake falling from her grasp. She did not hear it clatter to the floor, as she was already dead when she joined it a moment later.

A cat broke from the shadows. Sniffing at her body, it let out a plaintive meow.

'Your mistress has not died in vain,' the man said, picking up the cat. 'Her death is only a small part of a much larger plan.' A door opened and a woman who looked identical to Mavis appeared.

'She is dead?' the woman asked.

The man nodded. 'Go to the house and familiarize yourself with it,' he instructed. 'You must know every corner of it by the time they arrive.' As the woman left, the scarred man brought the cat to his face and read the name on the collar.

'Never mind, Felix,' he said. 'Would kitty like some milk?'

Chapter Two

'Sydney,' Brodie said. 'I didn't know it was such a beautiful place.'

We were halfway across the Sydney Harbor Bridge. A stiff breeze swept over the iconic landmark, but I didn't care. I'd faced death so many times that a cool wind was the least of my problems.

Five of us—myself, Brodie, Chad, Dan and Ebony—were directly over the glistening harbor. Chuffing across the water was a green and ivory ferry, the name *Queenscliff* emblazoned on her bow. A flotilla of sailing boats gracefully curved out of her path, heading out to sea. Leaden clouds nestled on the distant horizon, but the sky above was clear and blue.

We stopped.

From here we could see the famous Sydney Opera House with its white sails gleaming in the midday light. I wished Ferdy could see this, but being permanently locked in the computer system of *Liber8tor* made sightseeing a problem. We'd left the ship in a large park, the cloaking device engaged, a few miles east of the city.

'None of this rings a bell?' Chad asked.

The breeze caught at Brodie's hair. She was Australian, but like the rest of us, had no memory of her previous life.

She pondered the question. 'No,' she said, finally. 'Sydney's a wonderful city with a beautiful harbor and friendly people, but I don't remember ever being here before.'

'Maybe you haven't,' Dan said. 'Australia's a big place.'

Australia *was* a big place. Until we flew here in *Liber8tor*, I don't think any of us had any idea exactly how big. We had shaken off Agency pursuit ships—known as Flex craft—thanks to a new device built by Ferdy. His genius mind had once again worked out a way to make *Liber8tor*'s cloaking device invisible to The Agency. How long it would work, like so many other things in this crazy world, was impossible to know.

'That's true,' Brodie said. 'I could have lived in a million places in this country. A different capital city, maybe, or someone in the outback.'

We'd flown over the outback, a huge region of red dirt and scrubland that seemed to go on forever. It had been a surprise to us all. The unchanging landscape, spreading from one horizon to the opposite, had looked like the surface of another world.

Coming to a halt, Chad accidently bumped into Brodie and apologized. Swallowing, I glanced away. I should have felt relaxed, but I'd been on edge ever since our last adventure where we'd traveled in time and seen what our futures held; Chad and Brodie were together, and had a child, leaving me a bitter old man.

We had changed history. The events of that terrible future might never eventuate, but it was hard to forget. I had to focus on the now, but that was easier said than done.

Taking a deep breath, I turned to the gray structure around us. The Sydney Harbor Bridge had eight lanes, with rail lines and a dedicated bike track on the other side. Our side was pedestrians only. Men were working on the metalwork high overhead. I remembered Ferdy telling us the bridge was being constantly repainted, as part of the process to keep it protected from the elements, particularly the salt air.

I had to forget about Chad and Brodie. We were momentarily free of The Agency, and freedom had to be enjoyed. If only it could stay like this—

Ka-boom!

The bridge shuddered violently.

'What the—?' Chad started.

A fiery blast had struck the opposite side. Cars slammed into each other, cyclists came off their bikes and a train skidded off the tracks. Tourists screamed and grabbed handrails for support as the bridge shook, as if hit by an earthquake.

'Up there!' Brodie yelled.

Three black figures flew across the sky, nimbly skirted the web of trusses to land in the middle of the bridge. The letter *E*, in a circle, was printed on their costumes. Beneath the logos were numbers—One, Two and Three.

Dan started. 'They must be—'

'—E-Group,' I said.

E-Group were a worldwide terrorist organization dedicated to the destruction of the world economy. They weren't mods like us. Instead, their powers came from their high-tech uniforms, ironic considering they were against technology and everything that came with it. The group had attacked over a dozen famous landmarks worldwide. It looked like the Sydney Harbor Bridge was next.

One raised a hand and pointed it in our direction.

'Down!' I screamed.

A bolt of power flew through the air and would have killed us—if not for the titanium wall thrown up by Ebony. It held, but only just. Two fired a bolt at the bridge itself, cutting the deck in two. Cars tumbled towards the gap.

'They're using some kind of laser,' Ebony yelled.

'No kidding!' Chad responded.

'You go after them!' Brodie yelled. 'We'll look after the people.'

Taking to the air, I fired a blast of air at Three.

He was thrown backwards, but Two followed up with a fiery blast of his own. I threw up an invisible barrier of compressed air, but not quickly enough. The explosion sent me flying over the side of the bridge. For what seemed like an eternity, I fell towards the sparkling waters of the harbor. Then a blast of hot air hit my face and someone grabbed me.

Chad.

He had been trying to perfect his flying skills for months, creating a cushion of hot air for him to travel on. The results had ranged from competent to dangerous. At least this time it had worked.

'Thanks,' I said, pulling myself from his grasp. 'I'm fine.'

He looked annoyed, but simply nodded, releasing me to fly back towards the bridge. As he disappeared over the top, I saw something begin to tumble over the other side—a train.

Putting on a burst of speed, I threw myself under it, firing a blast of air at the locomotive. Halting its descent, I started pushing it back towards the bridge, but then I saw a door slide open. A young girl, clinging to a railing gave a scream as she fell through the gap. Catching her in mid air, my focus on the train lapsed and it continued over the edge.

Then I saw the metal of the train *melt* into the bridge.

How—?

Dan's head appeared over a railing.

'Just call me *Metal Boy*!' he yelled.

'I'll give it some thought!'

Returning the girl to the bridge, I landed near the others. Brodie was engaged in a fist fight with Two, or a more accurate way of saying it would be that Brodie was introducing him to her fists—close up. He was firing blasts at her, but you can't hurt what you can't hit. She was simply too fast.

Swinging about, she sent a roundhouse kick into his face and he went flying. Hitting the ground, he did not move.

The bridge gave an enormous shudder. One had taken to the air and was firing blasts at the suspension cables. It was only a matter of time before the weight became too great and the whole bridge collapsed. Ebony raced over to the deck and touched the road. A bolt of metal shot towards the upper span and linked. That would slow down the destruction, but wouldn't stop it indefinitely.

Chad flew towards One, firing icy bolts at him. A shaft of ice struck One's rocket pack and he lost power, crashing into the deck of the bridge.

I glanced back at Brodie. Two was now on the ground. That meant more than half their team was finished. But where was—

Three emerged from behind a crashed car. As he fired a bolt at me, I threw up a shield to block it, but he followed up with two blasts, aimed at the main supports of the overhead span. Twisted metal and cabling fell. I ducked, running for cover.

Using an abandoned car for cover, I fired compressed air at Three. He went flying and did not move again.

Ebony and Dan quickly went to work, reconnecting the deck of the bridge. As I took to the sky, I caught a glimpse of Chad working on the opposite span. He was melting shattered crossbeams together and freezing them to form joins. I went to the other span, using air to merge the broken pieces back together. This wasn't going to be easy. My powers were good at wrecking things, but not so good at putting them back together.

'Having fun?'

Turning I saw a woman in midair next to me. She wore a blue mask over the upper part of her face, and a red-and-white tightly fitted uniform.

'Not really,' I said.

'Mind if I lend a hand?'

'Please do.'

She pointed, and the two pieces of span melted back into a solid join.

'You must be Agent Australia,' I said. The uniformed hero had made the news several times in the last few months. 'That's quite a costume.'

Underneath that mask was an attractive woman, blonde with blue eyes, a few years my senior. It took me a moment to remind myself that many superheroes worked for The Agency.

'That's me,' she said. 'And you are?'

I didn't say anything as we floated down to the deck. Sirens filled the air as police vehicles and ambulances approached. Injured people were all over the road. Several had been killed. Traffic was gridlocked, and would stay like that for most of the day.

'A mystery,' I said.

'One I should probably be investigating,' Agent Australia said. She held out a hand. 'Thanks for helping.'

'Our pleasure.'

'You should probably be going, Axel.'

So she knew my name.

'Thanks for the advice,' I said.

I joined Chad and the others. We merged with the crowds and were off the bridge in a matter of minutes. We had saved a lot of lives today, but I couldn't stop thinking about Agent Australia. She had been on our side. Not everyone who worked for The Agency was against us.

'Where to now?' Dan asked.

'*Liber8tor*,' I said. Sydney was in chaos.

People had lost loved ones. Lives had been changed forever. 'We've had enough sightseeing for one day.'

Chapter Three

'Ferdy is pleased to see you enjoyed your time in Sydney,' Ferdy said.

'I don't think *enjoyed* is the way to describe it,' Chad said, rolling his eyes. '*Survived* is probably more accurate.'

We were back *Liber8tor*'s flight deck. The ship was our home, or the only home we knew. Dan was at the helm, Chad weapons, Ebony navigation, and Brodie science. My job was to monitor environmental systems, which meant I didn't have a whole lot to do. Reading the Tagaar language had become easier as the weeks had passed, but I wasn't ready to tackle the classics.

Dan had dedicated himself to learning as much about the ship as possible. I was impressed. For a young kid, he had already learnt a lot. He had Ferdy's help, but Ferdy was sometimes hard to understand. Just because you're a genius doesn't mean you can carry on a conversation.

'Did things go badly in Sydney?' Ferdy asked.

'Just the usual,' Ebony said breezily. 'Super

villains. Explosions. Collapsing bridges.'

I liked that. *The usual.* Glancing over at Brodie, I caught her eye and she smiled. I almost smiled back, but then I remembered things had changed. We weren't a couple anymore. That didn't mean we couldn't still be friends, but nothing was the same anymore. Despite her insistence that she had no romantic interest in Chad, I still thought they might end up together. And where did that leave me? Out of the loop.

'*Liter8tor* is receiving a message on a closed channel,' Ferdy reported.

'A message?' Brodie said. 'I didn't think anyone had our phone number.'

'It's on a channel used only by the Tagaar.'

'So the Tagaar are calling us?' Ebony said.

We weren't exactly on speaking terms with the Tagaar. Alien species lose a lot of brownie points when they try to invade your planet.

'The message is not coming from beyond Earth,' Ferdy said. 'It is coming from the United States, the town known as New Haven, to be exact.'

New Haven? That was the settlement established by the survivors of the spacecraft that had crashed on Earth. Species from a hundred worlds lived there, in permanent quarantine, while their status was debated at the United Nations.

'What does the message say?' Chad asked.

'*Come at once. We have urgent information for you,*' Ferdy replied. 'It is signed, *Tomay.*'

Tomay was one of the aliens Brodie and the others had befriended during the time aboard the Tagaar slave ship.

'It's a trap,' Chad said. 'Got to be.'

'Maybe not,' Ebony said.

'But what information could he have for us?' Dan asked. 'He and the other aliens are stuck inside New Haven like rats in a cage.'

'I don't know,' Ebony said. 'It sounds urgent.'

'It would,' Chad said, 'if it were a trap. It's a juicy piece of bait designed to draw us in.' He glanced around. 'You're not seriously thinking about going?'

'Ferdy,' I said. 'What's the status of the new

cloaking device?'

'Fully operational. Though there is one important fact you should know.'

'What's that?'

'It's a fallacy that the Great Wall of China is the only manmade object observable from space.'

'Thanks...that's helpful.' Ferdy was full of interesting titbits, handed out at exactly the wrong times. I thrummed my fingers on the console. 'I think we should go. It might be important.'

Chad looked like he wanted to argue, but he clamped his mouth shut when he saw the expression on my face. Sometimes friendship is like a piece of elastic; it doesn't take much to break it.

'Okay,' he said. 'We'll go.'

Night had fallen by the time we reached New Haven. As we circled the town, I saw struck by how much it looked as if it had been created out of spare parts. The ship the aliens had crashed in had been disassembled into three main pieces. Clustered around these were a hundred demountable buildings. It looked vaguely like a refugee camp, which, I suppose, it was.

'Anything on sensors?' I asked.

'There are lots of bits of information on the sensors,' Ferdy said. 'Atmospheric readings, wind velocity—'

'I mean, what does security look like?'

'A six-foot-high wire fence surrounds the entire compound. Three Agency ships are circling the perimeter.'

'That sounds pretty normal,' Brodie said. 'Not so many ships that we can't get through—'

'—and not so few that it looks like a trap,' Ebony finished.

'How are our weapons?' I asked.

'Fully operational,' Chad said. 'I'm ready to blast anything that moves.' We all stared at him. 'Squirrels are safe.'

Ebony scanned her controls. 'There isn't enough room to put down inside the compound,' she said. 'But there's a small clearing a mile west.'

'Are we still receiving the signal?' I asked.

'Loud and clear,' Brodie reported. 'It's a

homing beacon. I can relay it to our wrist communicators.'

'Then let's do it.'

Liber8tor swept through the darkness to a break in the forest. It didn't look big enough to accommodate the ship, but Dan got us down without difficulty. As we headed for the exit, he started to climb from his seat.

'Not you,' Chad said.

'Why not?'

Dan had a chip on his shoulder because of his age.

'We need you here,' Ebony said. '*Liber8tor*'s got to be ready to take off in case of trouble.'

Reluctantly, he agreed. We left the ship and found a small trail leading towards town. New Haven was easy to spot in the dark. It was the only illuminated place for miles around. The settlement was quiet—it was almost midnight—but there was still an armed guard walking the boundary. We waited till he turned a corner before advancing.

Racing to the fence, Ebony placed her hand on

the ground and turned it to oxygen, creating a tunnel. After we climbed under the fence, she placed her hand on the ground again. While she couldn't create something as complex as dirt, she could create a single element. She turned the hole into carbon. No-one would notice any difference it they didn't look too closely.

Brodie led the way. Following the flashing light on her wrist communicator, we moved silently through the camp. There were no guards. With the perimeter surrounded, they probably didn't think the interior needed watching too.

Unless this whole thing was a trap, in which case we would need to fight for our lives.

Reaching the center of town, Brodie paused, examining her communicator. 'This is it,' she said. 'Tomay should be here.'

Almost as if on cue, a shadow broke from a doorway. The alien man known as Tomay stepped out, waving us over. Covered in a fine brown fur, he was tall with a snub nose.

'Thank you for coming,' he said.

'It wasn't easy,' Chad grumbled. 'We're on every wanted poster from here to Tagaar.'

He led us into a single-room building. It looked like it was made to accommodate thirty people, but the only other occupant was an alien woman, vaguely snake-like in appearance.

'Bax,' Ebony said. 'It's nice to see you.'

'And you as well,' she replied. 'Thank you for coming. We did not know how long you would take.'

'We have a Tagaar warship,' I said. 'We've christened it *Liber8tor*. It takes us wherever we need to go—and fast.'

We sat around a meeting table. I was worried about guards, but Tomay quickly allayed our concern.

'They don't enter the camp,' he said. 'Your United Nations has decreed New Haven to be independent territory.'

'Like its own country?' Brodie asked.

'Almost, but not quite. The United States is not so ready to give up its territory, even to us. But we are left alone, and given supplies when requested.'

'There have been quite a few changes,' Bax

said. 'I'm not sure if you're aware of everything that has happened.'

'Maybe you can fill us in,' I said.

What she had to say showed me how out of the loop we were. Each branch of The Agency used to have a Bakari working with them. Then one morning every single Bakari vanished. No goodbyes. No explanations. They were just simply gone. It meant The Agency was now on its own. As was Earth. It was a disconcerting thought.

The Tagaar had already tried once to invade our world. It had taken the combined efforts of every superhero on Earth to drive them away.

'There is an Intergalactic Union of Planets,' I said. 'Have you been in contact with them?'

'We have tried,' Tomay said. 'But our messages have had no response. We believe a dampening field is stopping messages from getting through.'

'Is that why you called us?' Ebony asked. 'You need our help?'

'Actually our intention is to help you,' Bax

said. 'A woman came here one day, desperate to speak to us. She said she had important information.'

'What did she want?' Brodie asked.

'She had seen a picture in one of your newspapers,' Tomay said. 'Taken when our ship crashed, the picture is not very clear. It shows a number of our people and other military officers.' He turned to me. 'It also shows you.'

'Me?'

Tomay nodded. 'The image was fuzzy,' he admitted. 'But it was enough to bring the woman to us.'

'What's so important about this picture?'

'The woman said she recognized you,' Tomay said. 'She said she is your aunt.'

Chapter Four

She said she is your aunt.

The words rang in my head. *My aunt.* It was almost too much to take in. I had wondered about my true identity ever since I had awoken in a hotel room, months before. My clothing had identified me as Axel. No last name. Just Axel. It may not even be my real name. The others had been through a similar experience, their memories wiped and given new identities. A day had not passed where I had not wondered about my family, my real identity, the life I had led before my modification.

I felt numb. I should have been overjoyed, but I felt nothing at all.

'Your aunt,' Brodie said to me. 'Someone who knows you from...before.'

Everyone was staring. 'Do you have an address?' I asked.

Tomay produced a scrap of paper with an address of a town called Halliford in Ohio. 'That's not far from here,' I said absently. 'We could be there in an hour.'

'Was there anything else?' Chad asked Tomay. 'Did the woman say anything about the rest of us?'

'No.'

'We should probably leave,' I said. 'It's not safe to stay.'

'I hope this is good news for you,' Bax said.

'It is,' I said. 'The best.'

We said our goodbyes and crept through the settlement without speaking. I tried to stay alert for guards, but my brain wouldn't work. My stomach was a hive of anxiety.

The place where we had passed under the fence looked the same. Within seconds we were on the other side.

Bang!

Ebony cried out. Turning the corner, the guard had spotted us at the last moment. Chad threw up an ice wall as another shot rang out, and it bounced off. We raced down the trail, bullets stinging the undergrowth like bees.

'Are you all right?' I asked Ebony.

'I think so,' she said. 'It's just a flesh wound.'

Reaching *Liber8tor*, Dan had us in the air in seconds.

'There are three Flex craft approaching,' Ferdy reported. 'They will be in firing range within one minute.'

'They can't see us,' Chad said, looking alarmed. 'Can they?'

'Ferdy does not believe so.'

Within minutes we would be miles away. Looking at the makeshift town, I thought about what Tomay had told me. The whole thing could be a complete accident. The photo wasn't clear. Maybe the woman claiming to be my aunt had mistaken me for—

'One of the Flex craft has fired,' Ferdy said.

'On what?' Brodie asked. 'We're not visible.' She stabbed at her console. 'I'm raising shields.'

The *Liber8tor* was rocked by a blast.

'We're visible to them!' Dan said.

'Can you get us out of here?' I asked.

'I'm trying.'

'Ferdy,' Ebony said, 'do you have any idea how they've penetrated our cloaking device?'

'It appears to be completely operational,' Ferdy said. 'However, the trajectory of the missile followed *Liber8tor*'s heat signature.'

Liber8tor's engine produced heat just like any other, emitting it via exhaust manifolds at the base of the ship. The missile must have followed the heat trail.

'Any ideas?' I asked.

'I've got one,' Dan said. 'But you may not like it.'

He threw the ship into a sharp ascent. Was he planning to outrace The Agency ships? Our shields might not last that long. Another missile hit the shields and we shuddered.

'Shields are down to seventy percent,' Brodie said.

Dan leveled out, increased speed again. 'On my mark, Ferdy' he said, 'cut all power except life support and sensors.'

'Dan,' Ferdy said, 'that will mean—'

'I know what it means,' he said, tightly gripping the control column. 'Hang on.'

Throwing *Liber8tor* into a tight spiral, I was glad I had eaten a small meal. Glancing over at Ebony, she gave me a sickly smile. I remembered she had asked for seconds at lunch.

'Ferdy,' Dan said. 'Cut power.'

The bridge went dark except for emergency lighting, casting everyone's faces in an eerie crimson glow. The ship fell, slowly at first, and then picked up speed. I understood was Dan was trying to do. Without a heat trail, The Agency ships had nothing to follow.

'We are at 20,000 feet and falling,' Ferdy said. 'Nineteen thousand.'

'Are the Flex ships following?' Brodie asked.

'They are combing the area without success. Eighteen thousand.'

'This may have worked,' I said.

'Hopefully,' Brodie said.

'Seventeen thousand,' Ferdy said. 'Sixteen thousand.'

'We need to break out of this dive,' Chad said. 'We're dropping like a stone.'

'Not yet,' Dan replied. 'Just a bit longer.'

'Where are The Agency ships now, Ferdy?'

'They are still where we left them,' Ferdy said. 'We are at twelve thousand feet and continuing to fall.'

'Restart the engines,' Chad said.

'Belay that order,' Dan said.

'Belay that order?' Chad looked at Dan as if he'd grown a second head. 'Where did you get— forget it, just restart the engines.'

'Don't restart the engines,' Dan said.

The engines stayed off.

I cleared my throat. 'Altitude?'

'Six thousand feet.'

'Dan?' I said.

'Not yet,' he said. 'Ferdy, tell me when we're at one thousand feet.'

'One thous—' Chad looked like he was choking. 'Ferdy! Restart the engines!'

'Dan is *Liber8tor*'s helmsman,' Ferdy said.

'Four thousand feet.'

No-one spoke. It hadn't occurred to any of us that Dan—the smallest and youngest of us all—could override our commands. But now wasn't the time to argue about it. Not with death only seconds away.

'Two thousand feet,' Ferdy said. After what seemed an eternity, he said, 'One thousand feet.'

'Now!' Dan snapped.

The thrust pushed us so far back in our seats that my eyeballs hurt. Brodie screamed. Chad had been in the process of climbing from his seat and was thrown to the floor. A distant rumble came from behind. At first I thought it was an explosion. Then I realized it was a sonic boom as we broke the sound barrier.

After about a minute, Dan said, 'Ferdy, what's the location of those Agency ships?'

'They have lost us. Dan's plan has succeeded.'

Chad stood up, groaning. He started towards Dan, but Ebony was already in his way. 'Back off!' she said.

'Out of my—'

'I said, back off!'

She shoved him. They stared at each other without speaking. Then Chad dropped his gaze and made for the exit.

'Someone's got to be in charge here,' he said. 'And it can't be him.'

Chapter Five

I woke early the next morning, washed, dressed and made my way to the galley where I found the others gathered.

Chad glanced up from a bowl of cereal. 'Ready to visit Auntie?' he asked.

I shrugged. 'I'll just see what happens,' I said. 'It may all be a case of mistaken identity.'

Dan spoke up. 'Or not.'

Brodie asked if she could go with me, and I said it was fine. Saying goodbye to the others, we silently left *Liber8tor*. Dan had put the ship down in a clearing in some woods a couple of miles south of Halliford, Ohio. Following an overgrown trail, we reached a tarred road and headed towards the morning sun. Mist filled the fields. A redbird broke from a copse and flitted into the sky. It was so quiet it could have been the first day on earth.

I should have felt elated, or excited, but instead I felt a strange compulsion to burst into tears.

What's wrong with me?

'How do you feel?' Brodie asked.

'Great,' I lied. 'This probably won't lead to anything. A blurry photo in a newspaper doesn't mean a thing. It could have been Abraham Lincoln in that picture.'

'Probably not.'

As the road turned left, we spotted a homemade mailbox: an old dairy can, painted canary yellow, with a slot cut into it. Behind it was a farmhouse, set back a hundred feet, white, with a tin roof and wide eaves. A knee-high hedge and a flower garden surrounded it.

I suddenly realized my heart was racing a mile a minute. *This is stupid*, I thought. *I've faced aliens and super villains and bombs. Why am I afraid to face a bunch of country bumpkins?*

But I already knew.

It might mean the end of everything. An end to the only life I've ever known.

The front screen door swung open and a sixty year old women stepped out. She looked like something out of an old depression era movie. Dressed in a checkered apron, loose shirt and with graying hair pushed up in a bun, her mouth dropped open as she saw us.

'Adam,' she said, taking a faltering step. 'Dear Lord, is it you?'

Adam?

Almost falling, she yelled over her shoulder, 'Henry! Come quickly! Adam's here!'

Running over, she scooped me up in her arms and hugged me tightly. She smelt of lilac. Drawing back, she stared into my uncomprehending eyes. 'Adam?' she said. 'You remember me? I'm your Aunt Louise.'

'I'm sorry,' I said. The whole world was spinning. 'I...I've had amnesia.'

Louise threw her arms around me again. 'Dear Lord, you've returned Adam to us,' she said, tears in her eyes. 'Back from the dead.'

A man appeared on the porch. He came towards us, open-mouthed, stopping a few feet away.

'I didn't think—' he started. 'I didn't believe it, but it's true. You're alive.'

These people remembered me. They *knew* me.

I'd like to say there was a rush of memories, that my whole past life returned in a flash, that everything I had lost had been restored, but it didn't happen. I didn't recognize them.

If they *were* related to me, then the process The Agency had used had been terribly successful; Louise and Henry had been completely wiped from my memory.

Henry was like a stereotypical man on the land. Lean, clean shaved, graying hair, face tanned by years in the sun.

Louise turned to Brodie. 'Is this your friend?' she asked.

'This is Brodie...Smith,' I said. 'I've been staying with her family.'

They gave her a hug and she looked as surprised as me.

'Come inside,' Henry said. 'Tell us what happened. Where you've been. How you finally found us.'

The living room had white walls, floral floor coverings and old English pine furniture. Pictures sat over the mantelpiece. My eyes focused on one in particular.

Stumbling towards it, I saw a photo of a younger version of me with two people, presumably my parents. The man was taller. I couldn't see any similarity between us, except for the height, but I was the spitting image of the woman. She was attractive and thin, with a pleasant smile, and brown hair and eyes.

'What do you remember?' Louise asked.

I wanted to cry. Coming here, I had doubted these people knew me. Within seconds that had all been turned upside down. 'Nothing,' I said. 'I...please...tell me everything.'

Shakily slumping into a padded lounge chair, I waited as Henry went to get us lemonade. He returned with a jug and poured drinks. Glancing over at Brodie, I saw her lips were pursed, her eyes narrow. She was staring at me, but I could not read her face.

'Do you remember the accident?' Louise asked.

'No,' I said. 'Tell me what happened. Tell me

about...me.'

Louise took a deep breath. 'Your name is Adam Baker,' she said. 'You're sixteen years old. Your mother was my sister, Mary, and your father was named Tom. You lived on a farm in Kansas until earlier this year when there was an accident.'

'What happened?'

'There were floods. You and your parents were in a car trying to cross a river. According to the coroner, the car filled with water. They found your parents in the vehicle the next day. You were nowhere to be found.

'We thought you must have been killed too, your body washed away by the flood. Then I saw that picture in the newspaper. I thought it was you, but I wasn't sure. We've hoped you would be returned to us. Now our prayers have been answered. We know you've...changed.'

Changed. That was a diplomatic way of putting it. 'I've got powers,' I said. 'I'm sort of a superhero, but then you'd know that.'

'When we spoke to that alien man—Tomay—

he mentioned you and your friends. We put two and two together and realized you had gotten into some trouble. That the government was chasing you.'

'We weren't sure what to do,' Henry said. 'We gave our address to him, but we didn't know if you'd ever find us.'

'But you have,' Louise added. 'Now you have a home, you can resume your life. Maybe, one day, your memories will return.' She stared at me expectantly.

'I need to think about this,' I said. 'About all of this. It's a lot to take in. I'll come back tomorrow.'

Henry scribbled down a couple of phone numbers. 'Please come back,' he said. 'Don't just walk out on us.'

'Where are you staying?' Louise asked.

'In a motor home on the other side of town,' Brodie said.

'I'll be back,' I promised.

After a few more minutes of saying our goodbyes, Brodie and I were back on the road heading back to *Liber8tor*.

'What are you going to do?' she asked.

'I don't know, ' I said. 'I wish I did.'

Chapter Six

'They've been gone a long time,' Dan said. 'I wonder what's keeping them.'

He and Ebony were sitting in his room onboard *Liber8tor*. Dan often spent his free time playing video games in his cabin. He was up to level sixty-eight of *Zombie Moon*. With a bit more effort, he would crack it in the next day or so.

His other interest was studying the schematics of the ship. He had made up his mind to become an expert in operating the vessel, and had been learning more with each passing day.

But now he found he couldn't focus. He couldn't believe they might be losing Axel. It was like losing part of his own body.

'It probably isn't him in the picture,' Ebony said. She had a soft spot for Dan. The youngest of the group, he always seemed to bear the brunt of things. 'Anyway, even if it isn't, it doesn't mean he's going to leave.'

'Doesn't it?' Dan asked. 'What would you do?'

Ebony sighed. He had a point. She had wondered about her past every single day since acquiring her powers. Where were her parents? Were they still alive? She and Chad were Norwegian, yet neither of them had any memory of their past lives. They could speak four languages, but couldn't remember learning them.

Everything prior to waking up with superpowers was a complete blank.

Would she return to her parents if they found her?

'I suppose I'd go,' she said, thoughtfully. 'If I could.'

Chad's head appeared in the door. 'Hey, you two,' he said, 'what's happening?'

'Nothing,' Dan said, frowning.

'You're not still mad about that thing on the bridge are you, squirt?' Chad asked, grinning. 'I was just giving you a hard time.'

'You're not in charge.'

'Neither are you.'

'I got us away from those Agency ships,' Dan

said. 'Your butt would be in jail if it weren't for me.'

'I would've just flown away. Unlike you, squirty, I don't need a spaceship.'

Ebony held up her hands. 'You're both driving me crazy,' she said. 'And this isn't about who's running the ship anyway.'

'What do you mean?' Chad asked.

'I mean you're fighting because you're upset about Axel,' she said. 'And him leaving us.'

They stared glumly at each other.

'A few things have changed lately,' Chad said.

'You mean, like us seeing the future and knowing that you and Brodie could end up together?' Ebony said.

Chad reddened. 'That's not going to happen.'

'Maybe,' she said, 'or maybe not. We saw how things could turn out. Maybe we've changed that future, and maybe we haven't.'

'That future didn't include Axel finding his family,' Chad pointed out.

'If he has found his family,' Dan said. 'And

what will the rest of us do?'

'Do?' Chad looked at him as if he were stupid. 'We go on living. We don't need Axel. We don't need anyone.'

'We're better together,' Ebony said. 'Ferdy?'

'Yes, friend Ebony?' Ferdy's voice came from the loudspeakers set into the walls. 'What can Ferdy do for you?'

'I'm just checking to see if you agree? That we're stronger if Axel's with us.'

'There is always strength in numbers,' he said. 'And the largest pyramid ever constructed is the Quetzalcóatl Pyramid in Mexico City.'

'Thanks for that,' Ebony said. 'But I'm not sure that's helpful.'

'The whole universe is in a constant state of change,' Ferdy continued. 'Axel may leave *Liber8tor* to live with his family, in which a whole new train of events will be set in motion.'

'Thanks for that,' Dan said. 'I think.'

'There is another issue,' Ferdy continued, '*Liber8tor* is experiencing a loss in power.'

'What from?' Chad asked.

'Ferdy does not know. It is small and started some five hours ago.'

'I suppose we should check it out.'

'We'd better search both the inside and outside of the ship,' Dan said, thoughtfully. 'Then I'll run some diagnostics on the engine.'

Chad sighed. 'Need I remind you, pipsqueak, that you're not in charge?' he said.

'Neither are you!' Dan snapped. 'What do *you* think we should do?'

'Uh, how about checking out both the inside and outside of the ship. And then the engines.'

'Genius,' Dan muttered. 'Pure genius.'

He and Ebony started on the top floor while Chad checked the exterior. Dan knew a visual inspection wouldn't reveal a lot. The most he could hope for was to spot something out of the ordinary.

Astronavigation was a dome-shaped room with a control panel in the center. They had never used the touch display in case they blew up something by accident. It looked normal, so they kept searching.

The next few levels were crew quarters. There was a small training room below these as well as storage areas where spacesuits were kept. The Tagaar were physically larger than humans; if Dan or the others ever needed to use the suits, they could wear them, but with difficulty.

An armory the next level down held dozens of rifles. Dan had rarely entered the room because he had never needed the weapons. Nothing looked out of the ordinary, so they kept moving.

There was little to see in the galley. The freezers still contained hundreds of packets of K'tresh, a frozen food Dan had learnt to endure, but not enjoy. According to Ferdy, it was highly nutritious. Of course, Dan reflected, Ferdy didn't have to eat it, and they did.

The engines were below this, a complex fusion generator that Dan had only just begun to understand. Ferdy had told him not to feel too badly about his lack of knowledge; some of the best scientists on Earth were only now beginning to comprehend the technology.

As far as Dan could tell, everything was operational. He and Ebony checked gages and readouts on the computers. Half an hour later, Chad returned.

'I didn't find anything,' he said. 'The hull seems intact.'

Ebony frowned. 'What happened to you?'

Chad had a lump on his forehead. 'I decided to head butt the hull to see which was harder. No prizes for guessing what won.'

Dan indicated the controls. 'We didn't find anything either,' he said. 'Everything seems normal.'

Brodie appeared in the doorway. 'Hey everyone,' she said. 'There's something I should tell you.'

'What?' Ebony said.

'It's Axel,' Brodie said, her voice catching. 'He's leaving.'

Chapter Seven

Farewells are hard.

I didn't know how hard until I had to say goodbye to Dan, Ferdy, Ebony, Chad and—of course—Brodie.

Although I had been in turmoil when I left Louise and Henry's place, I had known in my heart that there was only one real answer. I was staying. It didn't mean I was staying there forever, that I would never see my friends again. But it did mean I had to start a new life by piecing together what remained of the old.

Gathering outside *Liber8tor* with the others, I tapped my communicator watch. 'Ferdy?' I said.

'Yes, friend Axel.'

'I'm leaving now.'

'Ferdy will be sorry to see you leave, but we will see you again soon.'

'Is that a premonition?' I asked. Ferdy's intelligence was so great that he could sometimes predict future events with great accuracy. 'Can you see my future?'

'Nobody can see the future, but we are friends. We will see each other again.'

I turned to Ebony. 'I know this seems like the end, but it's not,' I said. 'It's actually a whole new beginning.'

'I know.' She wiped away tears. 'I'd do the same thing in your place.'

She hugged me, then pulled away, staring at the ground.

Dan bit his lip and sighed. 'Hey Axel...er, I mean Adam,' he said, 'when are we going to see you next?'

'Whenever you want. The door is always open.' I glanced around. 'Just don't bring The Agency.'

'We won't.'

I turned to Chad. 'Hey man,' I said. 'Looks like this is it.'

'Looks like it.' Chad looked like he wanted to either cry or hit me. Instead, he enveloped me in a bear hug. Rubbing the top of my head, he said, 'You remember Yodak Prison?'

We had been confined there not long after we met. It was an utter hellhole. 'How could I forget it?' I asked.

'You saved me,' he said, swallowing hard. 'You put everything on the line and saved me when you could have left me behind.'

'I did what I had to do.'

'I don't know if I ever thanked you,' he said. 'Ever *really* thanked you.'

'You have now.' I put my hand out and he shook it. 'Just look after the gang.'

'I will.'

And then—Brodie. I don't remember if I'd ever kissed a girl before Brodie. I'd like to think that if I ever lost my memory again, I'd at least remember the feel of her lips on mine. There aren't that many things in life you'd rather die than forget. Her kiss is one of them.

'I'll walk you to the farmhouse,' Brodie offered.

I nodded.

Leaving *Liber8tor* behind, I didn't look back. I thought I would burst into tears if I did. My stomach felt heavy, my throat tight and my head dizzy.

The trees on both sides of the road hung over us as we walked in silence. The morning was bright and clear. The smells of horse manure and freshly mowed hay danced on the breeze. An insect buzzed in the undergrowth. A falcon coasted overhead.

For a moment, I wanted to be with it, flying away.

Why am I dreading this? This should be the most fantastic moment of my life, but I feel like I'm going to a funeral.

'How do you feel?' Brodie asked, sensing my inner turmoil.

'Not great. I don't know why.'

'It's a new beginning,' she said. 'But it's also an ending. Our group won't be the same without you.'

'You can come and visit.'

Brodie smiled wanly. 'It's a bit hard to visit when you're on the run,' she said. 'You'll have to keep a low profile.'

I hadn't thought about that part. My superhero days were over. No more fighting crime and flying off into the sunset.

This is all happening so quickly, I thought. But The Agency stole my old life. It's time I got it back.

Rounding a bend, the distant farmhouse came into view. It looked solitary and isolated, surrounded by fields. When I had first woken up with newfound powers, there had been a few stray memories of someone who I thought may have been my brother.

But Louise and Henry had not mentioned a brother. He must have been a figment of my imagination.

I felt cold anger, as if I'd swallowed a piece of ice and it were lodged in my stomach. The Agency had stolen everything from me and the others. It should be made to pay. Instead, I would spend the rest of my life running away, never truly free.

'You've still got your communicator watch,' Brodie said.

'I know. I can contact you anytime.' It wouldn't be the same though. She and the others would be having adventures and saving the world while I was—what? Plowing fields. Planting crops. Attending school. 'Maybe you can all settle down, too.'

'I'd like that,' she said. 'But I don't know where that would be.'

'It could be here.'

'I know. But what about Ferdy?'

Hiding Ferdy was always going to be an issue. Still, couldn't we put him in a barn somewhere?

What a horrible idea. Spending the rest of your life locked in a barn. Where were these crazy thoughts coming from?

We were standing on the road outside the property now.

'I don't want to go,' I said.

'I know,' Brodie said. 'But you have to.'

'Do you want me to?'

'No.'

'Then—'

'You've got to find out who you are,' she said. 'Who you *really* are. Maybe you'll come back to us one day or maybe you won't. I don't know.' She paused. 'But I do know this: you can't live wondering about a life that could have been. You've got to know, one way or the other.'

I nodded. Brodie leant in and kissed my cheek.

'I'll think about you every day,' I said.

'I should hope so.'

Smiling sadly, Brodie gave me another hug and turned away, tears on her face. As she walked away, I called out her name and she stopped, turning back one last time.

'I'll be seeing you,' she said. 'Adam.'

Chapter Eight

Chad peered through the window of his cabin. They had taken off again towards Virginia since Axel had departed. Chad had tried listening to music, but the sound seemed to be lost in a haze of memories.

Axel was gone.

He wasn't sure how that made him feel. They had been friends—good friends—until their journey to the future. Everything had changed after that. Axel and Brodie had broken up, and there was tension in the team that hadn't been there before. Brodie said she wasn't looking for a relationship, but Chad knew he still had strong feelings for her.

Was it love?

He wasn't sure what love was. Wise men and philosophers had been puzzling over that for centuries, and there still wasn't an answer.

'*Liber8tor* crew,' Ferdy's voice came over the intercom. 'Please assemble on the bridge.'

'On my way,' Chad said, tapping his communicator.

He found the others at their stations.

'The power drain on *Liber8tor* is continuing at an increasing rate,' Ferdy said. 'We must put down soon or the ship will run out of power.'

'What's our current location?' Brodie asked.

'Northern Virginia, five miles east of a town called Targo.'

'Is there somewhere we can land without being disturbed?'

'There is a forest outside the town with a clearing big enough to accommodate *Liber8tor*.'

'Take us down,' Brodie said.

Chad almost opened his mouth to argue, but he remembered the last time that happened. Someone had to be leader, especially now that Axel was gone, and surely no-one could lead the team better than *The Chad*?

The ship landed in a forest clearing. Logging had been carried out here long ago, leaving the clearing overgrown with low-lying bushes. Beyond lay an impenetrable wall of thick woods.

'Ferdy,' Dan said. 'Do you have any idea

what's causing the power drain?'

'Not as yet, friend Dan,' Ferdy said. 'Ferdy can run a full check of all systems.'

'We already did that, but please do it again.'

'Are there any houses nearby?' Brodie asked.

'There is a street less than half a mile away,' Ferdy said.

That's close, Chad thought. *Too close.*

'We should check it out,' he said. 'Make certain they're not likely to come this way.'

Once outside the ship, Chad breathed in deeply, inhaling the mingled scent of pine and fresh ferns. His eyes settled on Brodie. She caught his eye and gave him a sad smile. He felt badly for her. Hell, he felt badly for everyone. But they had to keep moving forward. Axel—Adam—was gone. They had to continue without him.

'There's a path,' Dan said, pointing. 'It must lead to the street.'

The path was a tangle of weeds. At the end was a dirt road with an old house next to the woods. It looked abandoned. Further down the road was another house, a well kept weatherboard with a tidy garden. An old cemetery lay opposite. Passing the rundown building, Chad felt a shiver dance up his spine.

They could use that place for a horror movie.

'Visitors!'

The voice came from behind them. They turned to see an elderly lady emerging from the bushes. She was in her seventies, graying, with a kindly face. Removing her gardening gloves, she pushed back a strand of loose hair and peered at them curiously.

'Are you camping in the woods?' she asked.

'Yes,' Brodie said. 'Just overnight.'

'You must come in for tea and scones,' the woman said.

'I don't think—'

'We'd love that,' Chad interrupted. The old lady seemed harmless enough. And maybe they could find out the lay of the land. If this part of town was pretty deserted, maybe they could stay a while. 'Let me help you.'

He picked up her basket containing shears and a few cut flowers.

'That's so kind of you,' the old lady chatted. 'I don't get many visitors out here.'

'What's your name?' Ebony asked.

'Mavis,' the woman said. 'Mavis Shaw.'

'It seems very quiet around here.'

'It is,' she said. 'It would be lovely to see more people, but the road isn't good and no-one comes out this way.'

A quiet area, Chad thought. *That's not a bad thing.*

He was already thinking about what Brodie had been talking about; a permanent place to call home. They had tried it before, but it had not worked out. Maybe this was a possibility, a quiet spot in the country, away from the hustle and bustle. If Axel...Adam...had been able to make a new life for himself, why not them?

Mavis led them into her living room. A cat, perched on a sideboard, darted out of sight.

Friendly cat, Chad thought.

'That's Felix. She's been awful skittish of late,' Mavis said. 'I'll fix you some lemonade.'

She disappeared into a kitchen, leaving them to settle into comfortable armchairs around a coffee table. The chair almost swallowed Chad up. He could imagine someone dozing here at the end of a long day.

Not only did Mavis own a cat, he noted, but she collected cat ornaments. Hundreds of them crowded display cabinets and shelves. Music played in the background, a drowsy jazz piece. Mavis had been cooking apple pie, judging by the sweet smell wafting through the house.

'Have you lived here long?' Brodie asked, after Mavis served lemonade and sat down.

'More than fifty years,' she said. 'My husband, Harry, passed away the spring before last.'

'Sorry to hear that.'

'We own the old Cooper place, too,' she said, nodding in the direction of the house they had passed. 'It's a beautiful old building, but people have never wanted to live there.'

'Why?' Ebony said. 'What happened?'

'John Cooper, the man who owned it, was involved in organized crime—the Mafia, some say. He and his wife, Maria, and their two kids, Tina and Joe, moved in there after he left the business. Everything was fine in the beginning.

'Then, one day the milkman went to deliver, and he found the previous day's milk hadn't been taken in. No-one answered when he knocked on the door. Eventually the police were called, but the family was nowhere to be found.'

'None of them?' Dan said, his eyes wide. 'Where did they go?'

'Nobody knows. Some think a rival gang traveled down here to exact revenge, but there was no blood in the house, and nothing to suggest foul play. It's as if they vanished off the face of the earth. Harry and I were as much in the dark about them as anyone else. When the house came up for sale, we bought it, thinking it would be a good investment, but we could never rent it.'

Chad sat back. It was afternoon now. The

parlor was warm, and the lemonade sweet. Mavis started speaking about her collection of cat figurines, a subject that Chad found as exciting as listening to static on the radio. He closed his eyes.

'Chad?'

Blinking, he shook his head. It seemed like hours had passed, yet it must have only been seconds. He must have dozed off. Brodie was glaring at him.

'Sorry,' he apologized to Mavis. 'I was more tired than I thought.'

'That's all right, dear,' Mavis said. 'I was just proposing something to young Brodie here. I was saying how nice it would be to have someone staying in the house. Rent free. All you'd have to do is tidy it up.'

Rent free. That was quite an offer, and they could try it for a while to see how it went. If it didn't work out, they could always move on.

'I suppose we'd better take a look first,' he said.

'Of course.'

The cat was now sitting in Mavis's lap.

Obviously it had overcome its shyness and was now purring with pleasure.

Following Mavis down the road, Chad saw the sun was low in the sky. It would be dark soon. They stopped at the front gate while Mavis searched her pockets for the keys. Chad glanced up at the building. It was really very dilapidated. A Victorian styled house, it had arched bay windows upstairs and downstairs. To the left was a set of rickety timber stairs that led to a small columned porch. A curved transom was above the double front doors with an ornately decorated gable roof above. The decorations were all in curved timber, once brightly painted, but now peeling like skin.

Chad could see why people had stayed away from it. Without even trying, the place looked scary.

The late afternoon sun cast a red sheen onto the building, bright spots of light reflecting off the glass. Peering at a window in the corner, he saw a dark gap between the curtains.

Something moved. A woman with black hair, her face unnaturally pale, glared down at him. Before

Chad could make a sound, her face vanished as quickly as it had appeared.

Chapter Nine

'Look!' Chad yelled.

The others looked up to where he pointed at the window.

'What?' Dan asked.

'I saw a person.'

Mavis smiled gently. 'There's no-one up there,' she said. 'Nobody's been in the building for years.'

'But I saw...' His voice trailed off. 'I thought I saw someone.'

'Just the light playing tricks on you, dear.'

Dan couldn't help but smirk at Chad's face as he stared up at the window. He didn't hate Chad, but he wasn't his favorite person either. The gate squealed loudly as they entered. The garden was overgrown and the front steps vibrated underfoot as they climbed the steps to the porch. Mavis unlocked the front door. The inside was in good order, other than some dust and furniture draped with sheets.

'Take a look around,' Mavis suggested. 'Tell me what you think.'

'The building's safe?' Ebony asked.

'Absolutely.'

On the ground floor was a dining room, living room, kitchen and library, with books still on the shelves. Many of the volumes were old. The kitchen appliances, including the stove, looked like something that would have been quite fashionable in the nineteen fifties.

The dining table was long and rectangular with seating for eight. Paintings of various scenes lined the walls: a ship on a stormy ocean, a fox hunt, a burning building, and open fields near a dark forest. Dan thought they looked creepy. A painting took pride of place over the mantelpiece; a family portrait of a rather overweight man, balding with an unpleasant smile, a woman at his side with long black hair, and a girl and boy, both blonde, who stared disconcertingly at the viewer.

How horrible, Dan thought. *That's going if we move in!*

He wasn't sure why the others always wanted a base. Dan didn't mind living on *Liber8tor*. Sure, the decor was reptilian and the food terrible, but it was a safe haven away from the world. It was *their* home.

The staircase was long and winding, and seemed to take forever to get to the top. Four bedrooms branched off the hall on the first floor.

Mavis pointed at another flight leading to the attic. 'No-one's been up there for years,' she said. 'That's where all the ghosts live.'

She laughed, but she was the only one who did. Dan thought they all looked a bit spooked, but Brodie tried to put a positive spin on the place.

'It just needs a little spit and polish,' she said. 'And then it would be a lovely place to live.'

Sure it'd be lovely, Dan thought. *As lovely as the cemetery down the road...*

At least the place was solid and dry, and he didn't mind the opportunity to have a little more room. By the time they reached the living room, he was beginning to think moving in might not be such a bad idea. Brodie was thinking the same.

'We could stay for a while,' she was saying to Mavis. 'And fix the house up while we're here.'

'That would be wonderful,' Mavis said. 'An old woman gets lonely out here by herself. Having company would be lovely.'

The woman handed Brodie a set of keys and promised to look in on them the next morning.

Chad swung on Brodie as soon as Mavis was gone. 'Have you gone crazy?' he asked. 'We can't move in here.'

'Why not?'

'Because...well, because it's an old house...' His voice trailed away. 'And when I looked up at the window...'

Brodie rolled her eyes. 'You must be joking,' she said. 'Don't tell me you believe in ghosts.'

'Of course not,' Chad said, reddening. 'But I did see someone up there.'

'It must have been a trick of the light,' Ebony said.

Chad turned to Dan. 'You didn't see anything?' he asked.

'Nothing,' Dan said. 'Of course, I am short and young, so who can trust anything I say?'

Clamping his jaw shut, Chad turned on Brodie one last time. 'What will we do about Ferdy?' he asked. 'What if someone finds the ship?'

'That's a good question.' She tapped on her communicator and explained the situation to Ferdy. 'Any thoughts about how we can keep you safe?'

'The cloaking device will stop the ship from being discovered,' Ferdy said. 'The power drain is still continuing, but now that *Liber8tor* is not in flight, it has slowed. Ferdy will continue to run diagnostics to pinpoint the issue.'

'But what if someone does find the ship?' Chad asked. 'The Agency has been able to track us before.'

'Ferdy can control the ship if required. And the onboard security systems are highly effective at keeping out hostiles.'

'So we can stay here a while,' Dan said.

'Indeed.'

Dan and the others returned to *Liber8tor* to grab their belongings. With Ebony's transmutation ability, she was able to create precious metals that they could sell—and did—on a regular basis. They were slowly accumulating the makings of a new life.

Returning to the Cooper house, they found Mavis had left a large box of blankets and sheets on the front door step.

'*Thought you'd need these*,' Brodie said, reading the note. 'What a lovely lady.'

'Yeah,' Ebony said. 'Funny about her cat, though.'

'What do you mean?'

'When we first turned up, it treated her like she had the plague. By the time we left, it was all over her.'

'Must be skittish.'

Once inside, they arrowed for their rooms. Dan noticed Chad grabbed the room furthest away from the one where he'd seen the face at the window.

'Not afraid, are you?' Dan asked.

'Don't be ridiculous! I just wanted a...smaller room.'

'Yeah?'

'Forget it,' Chad said, stomping off.

Stepping into his bedroom for the first time, Dan looked about critically. It *was* dusty, but it was kind of exciting to have a place of his own. A *larger* place of his own. Dragging coverings off the bed, he found the bed in good order. He made it and then turned to the throw sheets covering the other pieces of furniture: a chest of drawers, a wardrobe and an old rocking horse. They all looked like antiques.

He dragged off the last cover to reveal a cheval mirror—a tall mirror set on an upright frame that could rotate 360 degrees. The edges were hand-carved in a motif of vines and flowers.

'Wow,' Dan murmured. 'This must be worth a fortune.'

He was surprised to see himself full length. The mirror in his cabin on board Liber8tor was tiny, he rarely got to see more than his face. Now he realized he was taller and skinnier than he used to be.

Must be all that K'tresh, he thought.

Dan's attention was caught by a painting on the wall of the two Cooper children. What were their names? Tina and Joe. He frowned. It had been painted by the same artist as the painting downstairs. The two children, unsmiling, were staring straight at him.

'What an awful painting,' he said.

Gripping the edges of it, Dan tried lifting it off the wall, but the wire holding it in place would not dislodge. Pulling it one way, then the other, he struggled to take it down.

What the—?

It would not move. It was so large he couldn't see the hook attaching it to the wall, so he pulled at it, sliding it up and down, left and right for another minute. It stubbornly refused to come away.

'That's weird,' he said.

Still, he thought. Nothing an ax wouldn't fix.

Frowning, Dan stepped back from the painting.

What the—?

He hadn't noticed before, but the children's mother was in the painting as well. Standing between the kids, Maria Cooper held her arms protectively around them. She was glaring directly at Dan.

Chapter Ten

'I'm telling you,' Dan said, 'it changed.'

'When you weren't looking?' Chad said, raising an eyebrow.

'That's what happened. One minute she wasn't there, the next she was.'

Brodie peered up at the painting hanging over Dan's mantelpiece. It looked completely ordinary.

'Maybe you didn't notice the woman the first time,' she suggested.

'How could I not notice that face?'

He had a point. The woman looked so unfriendly she was hard not to notice. Brodie had tried taking the painting down, but it wouldn't come away and she didn't want to risk damaging it or the wall.

'You'll just have to put up with her,' Brodie said.

'Maybe someone would like to change rooms,' Dan said.

No-one did.

'You'll be fine,' Brodie said, eyeing a book

Dan had on his bedside table. '*Monster Attack*? I wouldn't suggest reading this before bed.'

Dan nodded, silently.

Brodie went to bed feeling worried, but slept surprisingly well. The next morning, over breakfast, Dan reported he had slept soundly—even with the strange painting in his room. Brodie asked Ebony to go into town to buy some cleaning supplies while Chad said he would go to the supermarket for groceries. Dan told them he would play *Zombie Moon* for a while.

'Hey,' he said, at their outraged faces. 'I need to make certain it's working.'

Targo turned out to be a small town about a mile away, with houses and shops lining a single winding street. After buying armfuls of cleaning supplies at a tiny hardware store, Brodie grabbed Ebony's arm and pointed at a restaurant on the main road.

'Bobby's Diner,' she said, reading the sign. 'I don't know about you, but I'm hungry.'

'I think it might be the place to go,' Ebony

replied. 'This town's so small it might be the *only* place to go.'

The diner was a red and white building with a faded neon sign over the front. Inside, the decor was classic nineteen-fifties, with silver trim around the bar, tables and seating. Pictures of Elvis and other rock legends decorated the walls.

'Nice,' Ebony said. 'I like some of the oldies rock and roll.'

'Really?' Brodie frowned. 'There was music before the year 2000?'

The owner came over and introduced himself, not as Bobby, but as Eric. An affable fellow with a neatly trimmed beard, he wore an apron as faded as the sign out front. He told them he had grown up in the town and had been running the diner for eight years.

'You like the town?' Brodie said.

'Wouldn't live anywhere else,' Eric said. 'Although it's quiet. Way too quiet for most.'

Which might make it ideal for us, Brodie thought. *Not many people coming and going. We could settle down without fear of being found by The Agency.*

It didn't take long for their food to arrive—a couple of 'Bobby Dazzler' burgers and some milkshakes. The music on the jukebox was some old song by Buddy Holly. It was bright and cheerful, but they were the only ones to enjoy it. There were no other customers and hardly anyone on the street. Despite being midmorning, the whole town seemed deserted.

'How are you feeling?' Ebony asked. She added, 'Now that Axel's gone, I mean.'

Brodie took a sip of her milkshake. 'Okay, I guess,' she said. 'I miss him.'

'That's understandable.' Ebony peered out the window. 'It's hard to believe he's not going to be around anymore.'

'He's not so far away. We can visit if we want.'

'You don't sound so sure about that.'

Brodie thoughtfully swallowed a mouthful of burger. 'I don't want to interfere in his life,' she said.

'After all, he's got a family now.'

'He already had a family,' Ebony said. 'Us.'

'It's not the same thing.'

'I think family is wherever you find it. I hope it all works out for Axel, or Adam, or whatever you want to call him. If it doesn't, then he can always come back to us.'

Brodie stared into her milkshake. She wanted what was best for him, but she couldn't help wishing that things wouldn't work out with his aunt and uncle. Finishing her milkshake, she excused herself to visit the bathroom.

'Don't get lost,' Ebony said.

Locating a door at the rear of the diner, Brodie found a clean bathroom, decorated in a blue-and-white check. After she came out of the cubicle, she peered at herself in the mirror over the sink.

I really do want what's best for Axel, she thought. *But it's not easy.*

She dried her hands and turned to leave.

Broooddie...

Brodie frowned. *That's strange*, she thought.

That sounds like someone calling my name.

Shaking her head, she went to the single window illuminating the bathroom, a frosted pane high on the wall. She listened hard, but heard nothing.

Unnerved, she started again for the door.

Broooddie...

Where's it coming from? There were no air vents. No other windows or doors. It wasn't coming from the toilets. Her eyes shot to the sink.

'What the—'

She peered down the drainpipe.

'*Brodeeeeee....*' the voice sang out. '*Brodeeeeeeee...*'

Brodie's throat went dry. It was some sort of illusion. It *had* to be. The water was just gurgling in the pipes somewhere and making a noise that sounded like her name. Her mind was simply turning it into something she recognized.

Except...

The sound was remarkably like Chad's voice.

She shook her head. What a ridiculous idea. Chad's voice coming out of a drain pipe in the ladies bathroom? The others would laugh their heads off when she told them. The mind could do all sorts of crazy tricks when—

'*Hellllppppp*,' the voice called. '*Brodeeeeee....hellllpppp meeeeee...*'

Brodie looked into the drain in horror, and saw only darkness, except for the reflection of the window in the water at the bottom.

'This is ridiculous,' she said. 'How...?'

Then something moved in the water.

Brodie had faced super villains, monsters, aliens and things that had no name, yet she had rarely been as frightened as she was now. Looking down into the tiny square of light, she saw a person splashing about.

And she recognized him.

'Chad?' she gasped. 'What...how...?'

Against all reason, Chad had been shrunk and dropped into, of all places, the sink of Bobby's Diner. Gripping the porcelain, she pulled it away from the wall. Metal broke, a pipe snapped loose, water flew everywhere. Dropping to her knees, Brodie searched the growing puddle of water.

'Chad!' she screamed. 'Where are you? How did you—'

'Girly,' a voice came from behind her. 'What the hell have you done to my bathroom?'

Brodie turned to see the owner standing in the doorway with Ebony, aghast, behind him.

'Brodie,' she said. 'What *are* you doing?'

Chapter Eleven

Shopping is the most boring thing in the world, Chad thought.

He rarely shopped when they needed supplies for *Liber8tor*. Usually one of the others went out to buy things, but it seemed that settling down meant a whole new redistribution of duties. He had been put in charge of food. If it were up to him, he'd be buying corn chips and soda, but Brodie and Ebony had given him a list of everything ranging from breakfast cereals to bananas. The list looked as long as his arm.

There are times you almost wish for a fight with a super villain.

'Eggs,' he muttered. 'Where do they keep eggs in this place?'

The girl at the checkout of Bill's supermarket looked young and bored. Chad had already asked her the location of two items. The first, she didn't know *where* it was, the second, she didn't know *what* it was.

Can't get good help these days, he thought.

There were eight aisles of goods. He could be

here all day. At least the supermarket wasn't busy. He had only seen an elderly lady buying tinned meat and a woman, carrying a baby, cleaning out a shelf of disposable diapers.

Muzak played over the store loudspeakers. It sounded like Kenny G. *That's what they're playing in Hell,* Chad thought. *Kenny G's greatest hits. And you have a shopping list that never ends. And a bottomless trolley that swallows everything you put in.*

He was taking this way too seriously. He just had to track down the last few items and he'd be out of here. What was left? Chocolate cookies, bread, a dozen eggs and tomato soup. Dan liked his tomato soup, for some reason. And Ebony had a thing for chocolate cookies. He'd always wondered what happened to the chocolate cookies on board *Liber8tor.* Now he knew.

Who'd a thought it?

Scanning the shelves, Chad shook his head in weary puzzlement. The food of champions. Tomato soup and chocolate cookies. How could they have stooped so low?

Grabbing half-a-dozen packs of cookies, he dumped them into the trolley. That should be enough to keep Ebony going for a while. Now for the soup.

Locating the tinned food aisle, he scanned the shelves until he located one that read *Tomato Soup*. There were two cans, but these were at the back. Chad reached into the narrow slot, but they were too far away. He needed a stick or something to drag them forward.

Through the gap between the two solitary cans, he saw two eyes staring back.

Yuk.

Chad swallowed.

They were not nice eyes. There was something hateful in them. They belonged to a woman with short black hair, cut in a straight fringe. She was staring at him with something like loathing. The whites of the eyes were ivory, with narrow bloodshot lines radiating from the iris. Without blinking, she stared directly at him as if made from stone.

Even more unnerving, Chad thought he knew them. He glanced away, pretending to examine the vegetable soup on the shelf below.

Where did he know those eyes? It wasn't anyone from The Agency. Maybe it was...

Maria Cooper.

A tremor of fear ran down his spine. He had last seen those terrible eyes in the painting on the wall of the dining room. *This is ridiculous.* Maria Cooper had been dead for decades and her ghost certainly wasn't prowling Bill's Supermarket on the main street of Targo.

Who had been on the other side of the shelf?

Looking up, he saw the eyes were gone.

Abandoning the trolley, he started down the aisle, but before he had taken a dozen steps, something hit the floor behind him.

A packet of cookies lay in the middle of the aisle.

I've got superpowers, he reminded himself. *I could burn this place to the ground or turn it into an iceblock.*

But he was still afraid. This was outside of his experience. First there had been the face at the window—which he had *not* imagined—and now he was in America's only haunted supermarket being stalked by *Maria Cooper*.

This isn't right, he thought. *Ghosts are supposed to hang out at houses. It's a rule. They're not allowed to stalk you at the supermarket.*

Rounding the aisle, he saw exactly what he expected in the next aisle—nothing. The woman had disappeared into thin air. But she had left something behind. A small gold object lay on the polished linoleum floor. A sense of dread grew stronger in the pit of Chad's stomach as he approached it.

Gleaming under the fluorescent lights was a golden earring. He had seen it before. Maria Cooper was wearing it in the painting in Dan's room. Chad swallowed. Dan was right. There was something creepy about the painting.

I don't believe this, he thought. *I must be losing my mind. There's no such thing as ghosts. They're as real as elves!*

'Excuse me?'

Chad almost jumped a mile in the air. He swung about to attack—and found himself face-to-face with an elderly lady. She drew back in sudden fear.

'I'm sorry,' Chad said, swallowing. 'I'm a little jumpy.'

'Is it the drugs?'

'Pardon?'

'The drugs,' the lady persisted. 'I hear all the young people are taking them.'

'No,' Chad said. The Agency had plugged him full of drugs, giving him super powers. Since finding that out, he'd developed an aversion to medicine. He didn't even take headache pills. 'Can I help you?'

'There's something high on the shelf,' she said. 'I can't reach it.'

'I'll get it.'

She led him down the aisle to a supersized packet of *Rice Pops* cereal. 'It's on special,' she confided. 'Only eight dollars.'

'What a bargain,' he said.

Reaching up, he grabbed the box and started to ease it off the shelf. He almost had it when it stopped—and was jerked back.

'Is it stuck?' the old lady asked.

Chad broke out in a sweat. He wanted *out* of this place. 'I think so,' he rasped. 'Stuck.' He gave it another tug and almost had it, but the box was yanked from his grasp. This time he saw what had dragged it away: a thin, skeletal hand with an emerald ring on one finger.

I know whose hand it is, he thought, resisting the urge to scream. *It's that woman. Maria Cooper.*

'Can you reach it?' the old lady continued, oblivious to his terror. 'I might get two because...'

Her voice faded to silence. Chad wanted to scream, but instead stepped back from the shelf. Struggling to keep his voice calm, he grabbed a smaller packet from a lower shelf and threw it into her trolley. 'It's jammed tight,' he said. 'Choose something else!'

Without another word, he hurried down the

aisle, grabbed his trolley and raced it to the checkout. Glancing over his shoulder, he expected the supermarket to look like something out of a horror film, with a dozen zombie ghosts giving chase. Instead, it resembled any other supermarket in middle America. Kenny G continued to play. Refrigerators at the back hummed contentedly. Everything looked terrifyingly normal.

Chad glanced at the boy at the checkout. 'The girl gone home?' he asked.

'Wassat?

'The girl who was working here.'

The boy frowned. 'The girl? I'm the only one working today.'

Of course you're the only one working today! Even the checkout chick is a poltergeist!

'There was...' Chad swallowed hard. Pulling money from his wallet, he threw it at the boy. 'Never mind.'

After the boy packed his groceries, Chad grabbed the bags and ran.

Chapter Twelve

Zombie Moon was probably the greatest computer game ever made, but only so many zombies could be killed before fatigue began to set in. Dan had been playing the game for three solid hours and his brain was frazzled. Finally, he put it aside, and decided to do something revolutionary—take a walk. The game was set up in his bedroom, and he had successfully ignored the painting over the mantelpiece the whole time.

While he and the others had not been able to take it off the wall, they had been able to throw a sheet over it.

Why am I so worried about a painting? He didn't believe in ghosts. They were just something invented by horror writers to scare people. And he must have imagined seeing the change in the painting. Maria Cooper had been in it the whole time. He just hadn't noticed her.

With the gaming console off, the only sound in the house was a slight hum from the TV and a tap dripping in the upstairs bathroom.

Targo was a surprisingly short distance from the house, and it was quieter than he'd expected. It really was a backwater, and didn't look like it'd ever been the center of the universe.

A small town doesn't seem like much when you've seen what we've seen, he thought. *Foreign countries. Aliens. The future.*

His eyes traced the stores lining the main street. Hardware. Supermarket. Pharmacy.

Thrilling, he thought. *This could keep me entertained for all of fifteen seconds.*

His eyes focused on an older stone building—the library. He arrowed towards it. While it was unlikely he could borrow any books—he didn't have any identification—at least he could take a look around. Ebony was always giving him a hard time about his gaming.

'Playing computer games means you're indulging in someone else's world,' she said. *'Reading puts you into a shared space with the writer.'*

Whatever that meant.

The lady at the desk glanced up. Elderly, with her gray hair in a bun, round black-rimmed spectacles and a severe face, she stared at him as if he'd interrupted her day.

'Can I help you with anything?' she asked, her name badge identifing her as Barbara.

'What time do you close?'

'Eight o'clock.'

What a cheerful woman, Dan thought, as he wandered aimlessly around the shelves. *This place needs updating. The only computers are for the library catalog and the magazines look like they came out last century.*

But what they didn't have in new tech, they made up for in old tech. The library had thousands of books, the stacked shelves reaching almost to the ceiling, with ladders on wheels joined to each shelf. Dan gazed around, feeling like a kid in a candy store. There had to be something here to keep him occupied for the next few hours.

When he did read, Dan liked adventure stories, so he went over to that section and leafed through a few books. After the incident with the painting, Ebony had advised him against reading *Monster Attack*, but he couldn't resist leafing through a novel entitled *Zombie Airship*. Settling into a corner, he was engrossed within minutes.

Hehehe.

Dan glanced up. What an odd laugh. Was it Barbara, the librarian? Peering through a gap in the shelves, he saw her desk was now vacant. Dan seemed to be the alone. *What a strange way to run a library.* Barbara had abandoned the building to the patrons. Sighing, he settled back into his seat and continued reading.

A dust mote floated down onto the page. Looking up, he saw a black shape draw back from the top shelf. The hair stood up on the rear of Dan's neck as he dropped the book and scrambled to his feet. For a second—just a second—it had looked like a flash of black clothing. But nobody could be up there. Not without making a racket and falling off. Unless it was a cat. They were incredibly agile.

Thud.

He swung about in time to see the shape leap from the top of one shelf to another. *That's no cat!* Dan's heart started thudding as he realized the shape had borne a frightening resemblance to the kid in the painting in his room, Joe Cooper.

This is crazy, Dan thought. *I'm out of here.*

He raced down an aisle to the reception desk, but the exit was gone. *Where is it? The door was over here.*

'Hello?' he called. 'Barbara? Librarian! I need to get out of here.'

Hehehehe.

Dan felt a strange mixture of terror and fury. He had superpowers. With his power to bend and control metals, he could tear this building apart. But that was against mortal enemies. Would his powers work against a ghostly child?

Something came flying through the air and slammed into his forehead. A book. Tears sprang to his eyes.

'I don't know what you are,' Dan yelled, his voice high, 'but you're not pushing me around.'

Creeping around the shelves, he could see no sign of the ghostly kid or Barbara. Or the front door.

This can't be real, Dan thought. *This kid can't just make a door disappear.*

Thwak!

Another book slammed into the rear of Dan's head. He spun around. Using his powers, he pushed the nearest bookshelf back. With an almighty crash, it toppled over into the next shelf, sending books tumbling to the floor.

The black shape leapt from the top of one shelf to the next.

Barbara, who ran the library, was going to be furious, but Dan was past caring. He focused on the shelf the ghostly kid had leapt onto and pushed it over. This time the effect was even more catastrophic. It slammed into the next shelf which toppled into the one after.

Crash! Crash! Crash!

Like a row of dominoes, the shelves continued to fall until a dozen of them lay in a chaotic mess on the floor. It looked like something out of the blitz.

And still there was no sign of the kid, the librarian or the exit.

Dan swallowed hard. This was freaky. Somehow this kid was circumventing the laws of physics. How could Dan defeat such a creature?

Whack!

Dan rubbed the back of his head. He peered across the piles of books and smashed shelving without success. Joe Cooper was nowhere to be seen. Glancing down at the book that had hit him, Dan saw it had fallen open. With shaking hands, he picked it up and read:

Another book slammed into the rear of Dan's head. He spun around. Using his powers, he pushed the nearest bookshelf back. With an almighty crash, it toppled over into the next shelf, sending books tumbling to the floor.

The black shape leapt from the top of one shelf to the next.

Dan's mouth went dry. This wasn't possible. How could he be inside the book?

'Dannnnn...'

He looked up, his heart beating like engine pistons. Something was moving under the huge mound of books—towards him. Dan spied a metal brace that had broken off the shelving. Lifting it with his mind, he used it as a spear and slammed it into the moving mound. The shape under the books squealed like a pig, but kept moving about. Dan stabbed again and again with the makeshift weapon.

Finally, when it was motionless, Dan crept over to the shape and carefully pulled back the books until he caught sight of a bloodied hand.

'No,' he said. 'That's not possible.'

Clawing back some more books, he stared down into a face he knew all too well. His own eyes, dull and lifeless, looked back at him. An exact copy of himself lay buried under the books, crumpled pages stuffed in his mouth.

'Good heavens!'

Dan looked up in shock. Miraculously, he was standing before one of the shelves. The library was completely intact. None of the shelves had fallen over. Every book was in its place. Barbara, the librarian, was standing before him with a look of utter horror on her face.

'What on earth are you doing with that book?' she demanded. 'Get out of my library!'

Trying to speak, Dan realized he had something in his mouth. *Oh no!* They were pages from the book he had been reading—*Zombie Airship*. Spitting them out, he tried explaining to the woman, but she was holding a large stapler in her hand, ready to use it as a weapon.

As Dan stumbled from the library, the elderly librarian yelled one last thing at him.

'And don't come back!'

Chapter Thirteen

'I'm telling you,' Brodie said, 'I could hear Chad's voice. I didn't imagine it!'

She and Ebony were back in the kitchen of the Cooper house. Before leaving the diner, Ebony had pushed money into the owner's hands to pay for Brodie's damage. He had not looked happy, telling them they were lucky he wasn't calling the police.

'Maybe it just sounded like Chad's voice,' Ebony said.

'But I saw him!' Brodie continued. 'He was in the water at the bottom, splashing around.'

'Splashing around? In the drainpipe? Are you sure it wasn't a bug?'

'A bug?'

'An insect? Stuck in the drain pipe?'

Brodie looked at her as if she were mad. 'You're telling me I can't tell the difference between Chad and an insect?' she said.

'The last time I checked,' Ebony said, 'Chad couldn't fit into a drainpipe.'

At that moment, the front door flew open and

Chad appeared. 'Okay,' he said. 'I've got something weird to tell you.'

'You think you've got something weird,' Brodie said.

Ebony and Brodie listened as Chad described his experience at the supermarket. The hairs on Ebony's neck rose as he told them about the hand holding onto the cereal packet. Although nothing had happened to her, it sounded like Brodie and Chad had endured similar experiences.

'There's something wrong here,' Ebony said, thoughtfully. 'Not just with this house, but in the town as well.'

'I think we should leave,' Brodie said.

'Agreed,' Chad said. 'Let's grab Dan and go.'

But they found a note from Dan, saying he had gone into town.

'Then we'll pack our stuff in the meantime,' Ebony said. 'And be ready when he returns.'

Ebony went to her room, feeling scared and disturbed. She didn't like unexplained events, things that didn't stick to the laws of nature. Despite the aliens and super villains they had faced, when she had nightmares, she dreamt of ghosts, goblins and monsters. Things that went bump in the night were always her greatest fear.

It only took her a moment to pack her bag. She wondered if Ferdy was all right. Tapping her communicator watch, she got only static.

That's a worry, she thought. *At this range the signal should be excellent.*

Picking up her bag, she started towards the door, but one of her feet caught. *What—?* Glancing down she saw it had sunk an inch into the floorboards.

That's not possible, she thought.

'Hey!' she yelled. 'Help!'

Now her other foot was stuck and she was sinking into the floor. Ebony screamed. She tried turning the floorboards to air, but nothing happened. *My powers aren't working*, she thought. *This is impossible!*

Her powers never failed. It was far more difficult turning something that was a multitude of elements into a single element, but she could still do it with enough focus. She concentrated again on the floorboards.

Nothing!

Ebony screamed again, but now she realized her voice sounded leaden in the room, as if it were muffled. The others couldn't hear her!

'Chad!' she screamed. 'Brodie!'

It was no use. The floor was up to her chest, and then her chin. Taking a deep breath, she watched in horror as the floorboards slipped past her face. Then she was falling. Endlessly. Darkness surrounded her, filled by a terrible laughter that came from all directions.

Hehehehehe...

It's impossible, she thought. *Impossible.*

Ebony closed her eyes. When she opened them next, she saw a leaden sky and a ship's mast. Salt water splashed her face. Wind clawed at her as she sat up. She was aboard an old four-masted sailing ship on a vast, stormy ocean. Lightning flashed across the sky. The sun was low, a single spear of light disappearing behind scudding clouds. The deck was wet with rain and salt water, the sails reduced to rags by the wind and the elements.

This place may not be real—couldn't be real—yet she had to treat it as if it were. Ebony focused on creating a weapon. With a huge amount of effort, she saw the atoms in the air coalesce into a sword.

Releasing a sigh of relief, she started towards the bridge on the foredeck. There were no crew on board, no-one guiding it across this vast ocean. The vessel was completely abandoned. Next to the ship's wheel was a metal plaque set into the decking. *The Eight Hands.* Putting down her weapon, she tried moving the ship's wheel. It slowly turned.

Cra-ack!

Thunder rolled across the sky. The horizon disappeared behind waves that heaved like mighty mountains. Through a gap in the waves, Ebony saw an island in the distance. The ship was turning, so she struggled with the wheel, aiming it towards the island.

Hehehehehe...

The laughter came again, carried by the wind. Snatching up the sword, Ebony's eyes searched the decks of the ship. At first she saw nothing, but then movement on the ragged masts caught her attention. A huge shape swung from one mast to the next.

What is it?

Shaped like a person, it was larger, and completely black.

Ebony swallowed. She had rarely felt so terrified in her life. But then her courage returned, like a flame fanned by the wind.

If I don't survive this, she thought, *then at least I'll go down fighting.*

Almost in response, the shadowy figure grasped a cross mast, snapped it free and threw it towards her. She leapt clear as it slammed into the steering wheel, destroying it. Grabbing the main mast, Ebony turned a section to air, severing it in two. The mast toppled sideways like a mighty tree.

Ka-thump!

Crashing into the deck, the mast flipped over the side, throwing the shadowy figure into the heaving water. Ebony went to the side but lost sight of it immediately.

Now she turned her attention to the shoreline. The ship was growing closer to a rocky platform bordering the island. *The Eight Hands* was almost on it. Grabbing a timber railing, she hung on tightly until—

Kra-ack!

The ship lurched wildly to one side, throwing Ebony to the deck. It sounded like the whole vessel was being torn apart. Lightning splintered the sky as she struggled to her feet and staggered to a railing.

The ship's bow was precariously balanced over the edge of the rocky platform. Water poured in through a hole in the vessel as waves crashed over the starboard side. The ship was seconds away from sinking.

Finding a place where some rigging hung over the side, she started down, but was still about six feet from the rocks when the vessel started to slide back into the water. She released the ropes, hit the ground and rolled.

The wind and the rain lashed at Ebony as the vessel gave a final groan before it disappeared beneath the waves. Soon there was only the top of the broken mast, and then this was swallowed by the eternal heaving sea.

Cold and wet, Ebony turned to the island. The sun was cresting the horizon. She didn't fancy being stranded on this rocky platform at night. Sliding on the wet rocks, she made her way to a narrow beach.

A dark forest lay beyond.

Ebony peered at the darkening horizon. She had no idea how she had gotten here, and she didn't know how the others would find her. It was as if she had fallen into some kind of side dimension.

I could be here a long time, Ebony realized, with a sense of growing dread. *Maybe even—forever.*

Chapter Fourteen

Ebony awoke to the sound of screaming. She sat upright, staring about in terror, completely lost. Then the memories came crashing back: the house, the ship and the forest.

The night had passed, giving way to early morning. Mist filled the forest, swirling about the trees and reducing visibility to a dozen feet. A distant creature—an ape, perhaps—was screeching. Its cries had woken her.

Ebony tried to make a titanium spear. With enormous effort, the atoms in the atmosphere slowly came together, forming a weapon three feet long, the end razor sharp. She let out a sigh of relief. For a moment she thought her powers weren't going to work.

Come and get me, she thought. *I'm ready for anything.*

Then she stood. *Ouch.* Her whole body ached. She was ready for *almost* anything. Ebony had spent the night curled up against a rock, with a palm overhead to protect her from the rain.

She sighed. What she wouldn't give for a shower. And a soft bed. And a big breakfast.

What she wouldn't give to be away from here...

The creature in the forest gave another high pitched scream and Ebony started in the opposite direction. Whatever it was, she wanted to be far away from it. Pushing aside ferns and palms as she pushed through the forest, Ebony heard the sound of running water. Quickening her pace, she reached a river. A huge log lay across it. The river was not wide—only about twenty feet across—but it was deep and fast flowing with smooth rock edges. Ebony couldn't see the bottom. She dreaded to think of what lived beneath the surface.

Another scream came from behind Ebony. The creature was closer. Starting across the log, Ebony dropped to her knees. The log was *very* slippery. Crossing with the makeshift spear in her hand made it even more difficult.

Okay, she thought. *Take it slow.*

A scream came again.

Turning, Ebony saw a huge shape moving in the mist. Three times the size of a man, it was covered in long, white fur. It gripped the log with two taloned hands.

Ebony started to turn, levitating her weapon, ready to hurl it at the creature.

'Don't!' she yelled. 'I don't want to hurt you, but—'

The end of the log lifted. She still could not see the creature clearly because of the mist, but she would be in the water in a second. And who knew what it contained? Driving the spear forward, she hit the creature in the chest. It roared in fury and lifted the log even higher. Ebony fell backwards, almost slipping over the side.

Throwing caution to the wind, she struggled to her feet and ran.

Only ten feet to go, she thought. *Only five feet—*

The creature twisted the log and she slid off the side. Her head hit the log and she saw stars. Then she was in the water. It was freezing. Rising to the surface, she saw the canyon walls slipping past.

I've got to get out, but there's nothing to grab!

Glancing back, she saw the monster, the spear still in its chest, loping through the fog along the side of the river. She still couldn't see it clearly, but it was shrieking with pain and anger. Swimming to the opposite side, Ebony tried to get a handhold, but the river wall was too smooth.

A huge spray of water, accompanied by a roar, was being thrown up hundreds of feet downstream. It could only be one thing—a waterfall.

I've got to get out of here, she thought. *But how?*

Then she realized. *What an idiot I am! I can transmute substances! I can turn this water into a solid.*

Trying to transform the water into silica, she realized she couldn't concentrate enough to make it work. If she could remain stationery for long enough, she could focus, but that was impossible. She spotted a rock in the middle of the stream.

Forty feet.

Thirty feet.

She stretched out and gripped the edge of it as she swept past.

Got it!

Copper, she thought. *Copper!*

Slowly the surface of the water began to transform to reddish copper. The river continued to flow under it, but she continued concentrating, creating a bridge from the rock to the riverbank.

Puffing with effort, Ebony pulled herself onto the makeshift bridge. She was exhausted. The water continued to rush past the other side of the river. Her bridge had formed a bottleneck and the torrent on the other side was tremendous. Peering into the mist, she saw no sign of the creature. Either it had given up, or it was sulking in the forest. For the moment, she was safe.

Gingerly making her way across the bridge, she pushed back her hair, shivering. She was cold, hungry and tired. And the day had only just—

Slam!

The bridge beneath her shook so violently she

was almost thrown off. Turning, she saw the creature in all its horror.

Covered in white, shaggy fur, it's arms and legs were long and articulated like a spider. It had seven razor-sharp talons on each hand. But it was its head—or lack of a head—that was most terrifying. There was simply a bulge across its shoulders. Beneath the bulge was a row of six eyes, and under this a ridged hole lined with stubby teeth.

Ebony stared, stupefied, by the bizarre creature. What insane sidestep in evolution had created it, she didn't know. All she knew was that she had an instant to stop it before it pounced. Dropping to her feet, she touched the copper bridge and focused on the section under the creature.

'Oxygen,' she said.

The bridge evaporated and the creature dropped, screaming, into the water. Clawing helplessly at the water, it was dragged away by the current.

Ebony caught a last glimpse of its hate-filled eyes as it was swept over the edge. Its scream briefly cut across the crash of the tumbling water before it was stifled forever.

Her legs shaking, Ebony continued to the embankment. She wanted to collapse among the ferns, but she knew it wasn't safe. Nothing here was safe. The only way to stay alive was to keep moving.

Cutting through the forest, she was relieved to see the mist was starting to clear.

Crash!

Ebony groaned.

'What now?' she asked.

A tree came tumbling down a hundred feet from where she stood. A huge shape was forcing its way through the trees, pushing them aside like matchsticks. It would be on her in seconds.

Something was coming.

Something big.

Chapter Fifteen

'Ebony's gone,' Brodie said. 'But where?'

By the time Dan arrived home, Brodie and Chad had already turned the house upside down. They spent another hour searching for Ebony, but she had completely vanished.

'What will we do?' Dan asked.

'Let's ask Ferdy,' Chad suggested. 'He may be able to track down her communicator bracelet.' He tapped his bracelet, but got no answer. 'He's not picking up.'

'Then we'll go to him,' Brodie said.

They followed the path through the forest to the clearing where *Liber8tor* had landed.

'Ferdy!' Brodie called out.

The ship was cloaked, of course, but when she didn't get an answer, the team started wandering about in search of it. It only took a few seconds to arrive back where they had started.

'The ship's not here,' Brodie said. 'Ferdy's gone!'

'He wouldn't just leave us,' Dan said.

'Maybe he left because Agency ships were closing in,' Chad said.

'And not tell us?'

'There may not have been time.'

Brodie didn't like the look of this. She couldn't imagine any situation where Ferdy would abandon them. Trying her comm bracelet again, she still had no success. This was bad. Very bad.

'Let's search the house again for Ebony,' she said. 'If we don't have any luck there, we'll head back into town.'

'How will that help?' Dan asked.

'I'm not sure, but whatever is happening at the house seems to be happening in town too.'

After another fruitless search of the Cooper house, they started back towards town. Passing Mavis's home, they saw her heading back inside after having done some gardening. They asked if she'd seen Ebony.

'No,' Mavis said. 'Maybe she's gone for a walk in the forest.'

'I don't think so,' Brodie said.

Mavis frowned. 'A number of people *have* gone missing over the years,' she said. 'It's been quite strange.'

'What?'

Now is not the time to be finding this out, Brodie thought.

'Clara Johnson's son went missing last year,' Mavis said. 'And a family of three—the Wilsons— went missing the year before. And, of course, there's always the Coopers.'

Brodie asked Mavis for Clara's address they continued down the street.

'If she weren't an old woman,' Brodie said, 'I would have yelled at her.'

'Would have been helpful to know weird things were going on before we moved in,' Chad agreed.

'I think we should meet up with this Clara Johnson. Her son's disappearance may be linked to what's happened to Ebony.'

They tracked down Clara Johnson's home, an old weatherboard, similar to Mavis's home, but with a lawn so green that Dan checked to see if it was plastic. An elderly lady, wearing thick-rimmed glasses, answered the door.

'We understand your son went missing some time ago,' Brodie said.

'That's true,' Clara said, frowning in confusion. 'What's that to you?'

Brodie had already concocted a lie. 'My father was a private investigator for many years,' she said. 'We've just moved into the old Cooper place. When I heard about your son, I wondered if we might be able to help.'

'That's very kind of you,' Clara said. 'The local police have been hopeless. Bert Wilmont, the chief, couldn't find a fish in a barrel.'

Clara led them inside to living room that smelt of lilac. Photos of a blond-haired boy decorated the mantle.

'It's been three years since I last saw Garry,' she said. 'He'd always had an interest in models and liked building replicas of the Apollo and Gemini spacecraft.

'He was pottering about in his room, building a diorama of the moon landing when he disappeared.'

'Did anything unusual happen?' Brodie asked.

'Not at all. He had his music playing. It was a lovely spring day. There was nothing to suggest anything was wrong. Or strange. After a few hours, I went up to see if he wanted anything to eat. He didn't answer when I knocked on his door.

'It didn't make sense. His music was still playing, and a half-completed model was on his desk, but there was no sign of him—then or now. Garry simply disappeared off the face of the Earth.'

Clara wiped away angry tears. 'The police conducted some sort of search,' she said. 'But they never found anything. My son was written off as a runaway teenager.'

'Do you have any theories as to who—or what—may have caused his disappearance?'

'I do,' Clara said. 'A company opened up on the west side of town, a scientific research firm, not long before he went missing.'

Brodie wasn't sure she saw any link between

Garry and the new business. The Coopers had gone missing years before, but it was the only lead they had. 'What's it called?' she asked.

'Cytron Engineering,' Clara said, giving them the address. 'But make certain you're careful.'

'We will be.'

After they left, Dan turned to Brodie and Chad excitedly. 'That Cytron Engineering must have something to do with Ebony's disappearance,' he said.

'Not so fast, pipsqueak,' Chad said. 'That's only a guess.'

'It sounds a lot better than ghosts.'

Chad shrugged. 'I won't argue with that.'

It only took a few minutes to reach the address Clara had given them. It turned out to be a modern residential brick house on the outskirts of town. It looked similar to the other buildings around it except for a business sign on the front lawn.

'This is the place,' Brodie said.

'What will we do?' Dan asked.

'Smash the door in. Chad can turn people into

blocks of ice while we pull the building apart.'

'Really?'

'No,' Brodie said. 'We're knocking on the front door. What else can we do?'

She knocked, but there was no answer. After knocking twice more, she turned to the others. 'Looks like no-one's home,' Brodie said. 'It's a shame these door handles break so easily.'

Snapping it off, she pushed open the door. The interior was quiet with a faint chemical smell. A lounge and kitchen were at the front with a staircase leading up to bedrooms. A door led down to the basement.

'I wonder what's down there,' Chad said.

'Let's find out,' Brodie said.

Snapping a light on, Brodie led them down a set of rickety wooden stairs to a concrete basement. Benches packed with pieces of machinery and computer parts lined the walls, but it was the device in the center of the room that captured their attention. The size of a small car, it looked like an electrical generator. A wand sticking out from one end pointed directly at the floor—or where the floor would have been. Instead a hole, wide enough for a person to fall into, led straight into the earth.

'Good grief,' Chad said. 'There's a light at the other end.'

Brodie peered down the endless shaft at a faint purple glow in the distance. 'I don't like the look of that,' she said. 'But it could have something to do with Ebony's disappearance.'

'Someone should go down,' Dan said, 'Chad.'

'What? Why me?'

'Because you can fly.'

Chad blushed. 'Not very well,' he said. 'And I've never tried anything like going straight down a hole in the ground.'

'But Ebony might be down there.'

'At the bottom of a hole?'

'Where else could she be?'

'About a million other places—'

'You're just afraid—'

Brodie cut in. 'Listen guys,' she said. 'This isn't getting us anywhere. There's no reason to think

Ebony's down there. I don't know what these guys have been doing in this place, but it may all be completely legit.' She peered into the hole. 'Well, mostly legit.'

'So what now?' Dan asked.

She photographed some papers on a nearby desk. 'There's names and formulas on these. We'll check them on the net and see if anything comes up.'

'We usually use Ferdy for internet access,' Chad pointed out. It was the safest option to keep them hidden from The Agency.

'We can try the library.'

'They don't have any technology post 1980,' Dan said. 'And I wouldn't go back there for a million dollars.'

'Then we'll return to the house and work it out from there,' Brodie said.

'Is the house safe?'

'Is anywhere?'

Making their way back through the building, they quickly scanned the street for passersby. No-one was in sight, so they started down the footpath.

'I feel kind of lost,' Brodie admitted. 'I wonder if we should ask Axel to give us a hand.'

'We can't go running back to him every time we need help,' Chad said. 'Although,' he added, 'we need to put Ebony first. What do you think, Dan?'

But Dan was gone.

Chapter Sixteen

Dan had been walking down the street behind the others when the footpath suddenly grew soft beneath him. At first he thought he had stepped in something, maybe something doggie and smelly, but when he looked down he saw the pavement giving way like quicksand.

'Hey!' he yelled. 'Help!'

But the world had frozen. Chad and Brodie were in mid-conversation. Chad's foot was about to connect with the ground. Brodie's mouth was half open as if speaking. Beyond them, a bird was caught in midflight while high above, a plane was motionless painted on the sky.

'Brodie!' he screamed, as he sunk further into the pavement. 'Chad! Help! Help!'

But now it was up to his waist, his chest and then his neck. He gave one final cry as he sunk beneath the surface, and darkness surrounded him on all sides. Closing his eyes tightly, he held his breath.

This is it, he thought. *What a crazy way to die! Swallowed by a footpath!*

But when he opened his eyes again, he found himself in an open field, surrounded by lush, green grass. The sun was low in the sky and the air cold, and it was early morning. Hills and fog enshrouded valleys receded into the distance. The scene would have been idyllic if he hadn't been brought here against his will.

Where am I?

The only answer was a distant howl that split the air.

What—?

A group of shapes moved across a faraway hill. Dan's mouth fell open in astonishment. It was like some sort of old scene out of a painting of a fox hunt. A group of men rode horses, accompanied by a pack of baying dogs, except these horses had eight legs and the dogs had two heads apiece.

What is this place?

Dan turned and ran as the group changed direction—towards him. As they raced down the hill, the sound of the baying hounds echoed across the landscape. Dan cursed. If only he had metal! He was a superhero. With metal he could beat off those hounds in seconds, but without it he was just another kid.

But there was metal in rocks, wasn't there? Iron? Lead? If he could find a hill laden with metallic substances, he could fight off these creatures.

Descending into a narrow ravine, the sides rising steeply around him, the howling of the dogs momentarily faded. He focused on trying to find metal in the rocks, using himself as a human diviner. His ability to read and control minds may have faded, but he could still manipulate metal—providing he could first find it.

A thin stream ran down the middle of the ravine before disappearing around a rocky hill. Dan followed, splashing through the shallow water as fast as he could, although running wasn't one of his strengths. *Chad's always saying I should exercise more*, he thought. *I hate it when he's right!* A trickle of rocks came rattling down the hillside. Peering through the mist, he caught sight of a dark shape. A hound was almost on him!

He focused on one side of the ravine, trying to make it reveal any hidden metal. Nothing. Turning to the other side, he concentrated again.

Come on, he thought. *Come on!*

The rocks started to shift and crack, but the dog's frenzied barks were growing louder with every second.

It's now or never, he thought.

The rock split and a jagged dark substance floated into view. Dan had no idea what it was, but that didn't matter now.

A hound appeared from the fog behind him. It was even more terrifying close up. Not only did it have two heads, but its teeth were dripping saliva, its eyes crimson red. It splashed through the water towards Dan. Stumbling backwards, Dan fell, and arrowed the lump of metal at the dog as it leapt into the air.

Th-wunk!

It slammed into the creature, throwing it sideways, stunned. But it wasn't dead. The dog's two heads narrowed on Dan, its four eyes glaring in hatred. Preparing to leap again, Dan brought the lump down onto the middle of its back. Something cracked loudly, and the dog took a final shuddering step before slumping to the ground.

Gasping for breath, Dan realized he was shaking so hard he couldn't move. His legs had turned to jelly. He wanted to take refuge and not move for a month, but now he heard the baying of dogs. They were closer.

I'm a superhero, he thought. *That means I don't give up.*

He needed a better weapon. Clenching his fists, he focused on the lump of rock, using his mind to shape it into a spear. The edge was blunt, but within seconds each end was pointed and sharp. It would ward off anything that tried to—

Smack!

Dan hit the ground hard, rolling through the stream. A dog had slammed into him. Throwing out his arm, he shoved it back as two slavering heads fought to tear into his face.

The spear, he thought. *Got to use the spear...*

One of the heads drew closer, its jaws snapping only inches from his face. Dan focused on lifting the spear off the ground. He arrowed it clumsily at the dog. It struck the animal, wounding it, but bounced off. The animal swung about in confusion.

Rolling over, Dan focused on throwing the spear at the animal again. This time he struck one of its heads. As the dog withdrew, Dan staggered to his feet. He stumbled backwards, but the dog was already racing towards him again.

Pure instinct made Dan throw the spear again. This time it slammed into the dog's chest, killing it instantly. Without stopping, Dan pulled the spear out and ran. Ahead lay a steep incline, but that wouldn't stop him. Dan let the spear float in the air behind him as he ascended, his hands gripping the rocks. He heard another dog in the canyon behind him, baying in frustration as it struggled to climb the rock face.

Puffing with exhaustion, Dan reached the top and found himself on the crest of a small hill. He grabbed the spear and ran, the baying of more dogs ringing across the hills. As the mist cleared, he spotted a forest in the distance.

Maybe I can lose them in the woods.

He wiped at his face and saw blood on his hand. The dog must have bitten him, or he may have hit his head. He hoped the creatures were not attracted by its scent.

'Tarn thokay!' a voice yelled.

Dan turned to see a figure on horseback bursting through the fog. From a distance, the man had looked human, but now Dan realized he was an alien, a man with feline features. Spurring his horse on, the alien charged at Dan.

Throwing himself to one side as the horse tore past, Dan was struck a glancing blow and sent spinning. His head hit a rock and he saw stars. The spear went flying.

I've got to get up, Dan thought. *I've got to move.*

But he couldn't tell up from down. Everything was weaving crazily around him. He tried to stand, but couldn't focus. All he could see was the alien on the horse. The alien kicked the horse's sides and it galloped at full speed towards him.

Chapter Seventeen

Dan focused on the spear.

Fly, he thought. *Fly!*

The spear arrowed through the air at the approaching alien. Missing the horse by inches, it slammed into the alien's left shoulder. The man tumbled backwards off the horse, the steed kicking dirt into the air as it sped by Dan.

Jumping to his feet, Dan watched as the alien calmly removed the spear from his shoulder.

'Karnup tuap!' the man snarled.

'I knew you'd say that,' Dan said. 'Ketchup to you too!'

Dan focused on twisting the spear around the alien's legs. He staggered a few more feet before being tripped up.

Dan ran.

How do I get out of here?

The sounds of frenzied dogs was drawing nearer. Racing across the field, Dan spotted a break in the trees. Aiming for it, the forest quickly closed in around him. It sounded like the dogs were getting closer. He had to lose them soon or they would be on him.

Crashing through the undergrowth, tree branches whipped at him and shrubs threatened to entangle him. He had lost his weapon. Getting another one would be almost impossible. If only he could take shelter—

Will you look at that?

Ahead of him was a medieval church. What it was doing in the middle of a forest on an alien world was a total mystery, but it was somewhere to hide. Carved statues of angels and demons decorated the arch surrounding the entrance. The timber doors were wide open. Dan climbed half-a-dozen steps and hurried inside. The interior was gloomy, the only light entering through the narrow stained-glass windows. The pews were made of hard timber. There was no crucifix or sign of Christian worship. Nor were there any statues.

The doors were lockable. Closing them, he fixed a bar across and hurried down the nave. The dogs would be here in seconds. Dan glanced up at the stained glass windows. They were decorated with images of spiders and octopuses.

I've never seen a church like this.

But he couldn't worry about the architecture now. He needed metal, but there was none in sight. The walls and floor were stone. The roof was timber. The pews were nailed together, but there couldn't be enough metal in the nails to form any sort of weapon.

A thudding came at the door, followed by cries in the same alien language. The hounds were going crazy. Dan's eyes darted about in panic. There were normally exit doors scattered throughout a church, but the only way in or out seemed to be the front door.

I'm trapped, he thought. *I should never have come in here.*

The bar across the front door started to bend and yield. It cracked. The cries of the men beyond, and the baying of the hounds, rose to a fever pitch.

Dan looked about in terror. *There's got to be a way out of here*, he thought. *A way to fight back!*

The doors smashed open, sending splintered

timber over the floor. The men on horses burst through, the dogs at their sides. But now Dan was staring up at the ceiling.

'Metal,' he muttered. 'Come to me.'

With every ounce of energy he could muster, he focused on the nails holding the beams together over the alien's heads. With one almighty effort, he willed them to come loose. The scream of metal tearing against timber cut across the frenzied shrieking of the hounds, and the cries of the aliens.

A thousand nails fell to the floor, bouncing off the stonework. The men on horses and the hounds stopped, frozen, halfway down the nave.

Then the ceiling over their heads collapsed.

The roof fell in, hundreds of tons of ancient timbers, crushing everything under them: pews, men, horses and dogs. The roar was deafening. Dan covered his ears and turned away. Finally the timbers settled and silence fell over the calamity.

Dan coughed on the dusty air.

'Hmm,' he said. 'I think that worked.'

There were now a dozen ways out of the

church—or what remained of it. Dan clambered over stone and timber, and back out into the forest. He was just starting to breathe a little easier when he heard a ground-shuddering thud. It came from the direction where he had attacked the first rider. Another thud followed it. And another.

Something was coming.

Something huge.

Chapter Eighteen

An hour had passed since Dan had disappeared and Brodie was still reeling from the shock. She could hardly gather her thoughts.

'He was with us,' she said. 'And then he just disappeared.'

Chad was so shocked he actually looked ill. 'They're picking us off,' he said. 'One at a time.'

After losing Dan, they had returned to Cytron Engineering to see if Dan had somehow been transported into the building, but it was as quiet as ever. Back at the Cooper house, Brodie was trying to make plans, but everything seemed to lead back to one conclusion.

'We need Axel,' she said. 'Ferdy was right when he said there's safety in numbers.'

'I gotta agree. The more of us, the better.'

Brodie had already tried using her comm bracelet to contact him, but there had been no answer. That meant using the traditional method—a telephone. They didn't carry cell phones because they could be traced, so they needed a landline.

'We'll ask Mavis,' Chad suggested. 'She's sure to have a phone.'

Arriving at her house, the old lady let them in immediately. 'Of course you can use my phone,' Mavis said. 'I'm sorry there's not one up at the house, but it's never been needed.'

Brodie tried dialing the number Axel had given her, but no-one answered. She put the handset down thoughtfully. 'He's not there,' she said. 'I suppose I can call back later.'

They traipsed back to the Cooper house and sat in the living room. The four of them had shared this room a few days before. Now there were only two remaining. A shiver of horror danced up Brodie's spine.

It all started with this house, she thought. *We would have been better off never coming here.*

'I'll fly over to get him,' Chad said. 'I know my flying isn't perfect, but it's better than hanging around here.'

'Are you sure you can do it?'

'I know I can.'

Chad had once carried Brodie across a city when she was deathly ill. He had almost crashed a few times, but he had made it.

He cocked his head. 'Do you hear that?'

She strained her ears. A murmur of voices was coming from upstairs. Frowning, she said, 'It can't be Ebony and Dan. Can it?'

'We'd better check.'

The voices grew louder as they crept up the stairs. It sounded like children laughing.

Brodie swallowed. The sounds were coming from Ebony's room. Chad marched up to the door. 'I don't care if these things are ghosts or not,' he said. 'They're not kidnapping my sister. I'll tear this house apart if I must.'

The instant he opened it, the laughter stopped. Brodie went to follow him, but she suddenly found herself frozen in mid-step. She could not move.

'Chad!' she screamed. 'Help! I can't—'

Within seconds she was sinking down into the floor. She continued to scream, but Chad was stuck, as if time had stopped. Within seconds, she was closing her eyes as the floor rushed past her face.

When she next opened them, she saw ancient stonework, a carpeted staircase and high walls that were clad in crimson and blue tapestries. A single chandelier, with eight unlit candles, hung from the ceiling.

I'm in a castle, she thought. *Maybe this is where the others went.*

'Ebony!' she called. 'Dan!'

Her voice reverberated hollowly. Stained glass windows lined the hall, the largest being a battle scene at the end. Crossing to it, Brodie peered through the colored shards. Open country lay beyond.

Clang!

The distant sound of metal against stone rang through the building.

Clang!

Brodie crept to the bottom of the stairs. The sound was approaching—and fast. Whatever it was, wasn't trying to hide, as it raced through the castle at top speed.

Glancing backwards, Brodie saw a door leading from the castle. If worse came to worse—

A gleaming suit of armor appeared at the top of the stairs. The figure stopped momentarily, pausing to stare at her. A shiver of fear danced at the base of Brodie's neck. There was something unnerving about the knight. There was no sign of eyes behind the visor in his helmet.

He gripped the balustrade and leapt over the side to the hall below. *Crash!* It sounded like a dump truck crashing over a cliff, but the knight landed lightly on his feet like a cat.

'Hey, big fella,' Brodie said. 'I'm not looking for trouble. You just show me the way out of here and I'll be on my way.'

Drawing his sword, the knight started to advance.

'Or maybe not,' Brodie added.

He was lightning fast. Swinging his sword, Brodie ducked as it passed where her head had been an instant before. She dived forward, lifted him off the ground and threw him over her shoulder.

Hitting the ground, he rolled and was back on his feet in a second.

He's so fast, Brodie thought. *I'm not sure I can—*

The knight leapt at her, the sword extended. Brodie jumped to one side, rolled and ran towards the stairs. She gripped a balustrade, pulled it loose and swung it around just as the knight reached her. His sword slammed into the timber, stuck and Brodie performed a roundhouse kick to his stomach.

Connecting, he was thrown sideways, but his sword pulled the timber from Brodie's hand. She raced to the door, but it was locked. *Damn!* Turning, she sprinted for the stairs and started up. At the same time, she glanced back in time to see the knight dislodging the wood from his sword. Drawing back the weapon, he hurled it at her.

Brodie ducked, and it clanged into the stairs over her head.

That was close, she thought.

Snatching up the sword, she threw it at the stained glass window. It shattered, sending pieces of lead and glass everywhere. As the knight raced up the stairs, Brodie climbed onto the railing, balanced herself and then took a mighty leap through the air, crashing through the shattered window and landing on the grass beyond.

Ugh!

She had landed badly, twisting her ankle. Rolling, she climbed to her feet and started running, but her foot was in terrible pain. In the distance lay a small village. She might be able to take refuge there.

A huge thud came from behind. Abandoning the sword, the knight had leapt after her and was already on his feet.

Come on, Brodie urged herself. *Run!*

Chapter Nineteen

Brodie ran towards the village. The houses were adobe, with thatched roofs and small, crude openings. There was no-one in sight. It was probably a good thing. She didn't need anyone else trying to kill her.

Her foot was hurting, but her fear was greater than her pain so she ignored it, running faster. The knight was still some distance behind.

Rounding a group of houses, she spotted a barn. Racing through the open doors, Brodie scaled a ladder to the mezzanine level. The place was stacked with hay, but there were no horses.

Trying to stifle her breathing, she huddled among the hay.

The knight might pass by without looking inside. If he kept going, she could double back to the castle. Then she could work out a way to escape, providing there *was* a way to escape.

The knight's footsteps approached. Brodie saw him pause in the doorway. He seemed to be listening intently, although she wasn't sure he had ears, or even a head for that matter. Slowly entering, his eyes swiveled from side to side, and finally up. Brodie remained motionless.

Finally, he seemed to decide the barn was empty, and started to turn away.

Then his arm snaked out, gripping a pole that held up the mezzanine level. With a burst of titanic strength, he pulled it loose. Brodie screamed as the unsupported weight of the floor caved in, sending her crashing to the floor.

The knight's fist came smashing down towards Brodie's face. Jerking to one side, she avoided it, and it slammed into the ground. His other fist came down and she rolled again. Drawing back her legs, she kicked into his midriff and he went flying out through the door of the barn. She leapt up and sprinted up the street as he climbed to his feet.

He was slow, but seemingly unstoppable. Brodie grabbed a hitching rail for a horse, jerked it free and aimed it like a javelin. Flinging it with all her might, the makeshift weapon flew at the knight, hitting him dead center.

'Wow,' she murmured.

The rail had pierced the knight dead center—and gone straight through him. Gripping it, he tugged it free, revealing a hole in his chest though which Brodie could see to the other side.

How was such a thing possible? How could it still be standing?

The knight lifted the weapon and flung it at Brodie. It missed her by inches, slamming into the wall of a nearby house. The knight charged across the ground. Brodie remained low, waiting till the last instant. Then she sidestepped, tripping him over and jumping on his back.

Pulling with all her might, she tried to rip his helmet off.

I'm going to beat you, Brodie thought. *Even if I have to take you apart piece by piece.*

The helmet came loose, sending her backwards onto the ground. Tossing it to one side, she watched in horror as the remaining body swung about, somehow sensed her location and ran at her.

Once again, staying low, she gripped the

knight's arm as he swung it around, and flipped him over her shoulder.

This is getting tiring, she thought. *I'm running out of steam, but he doesn't slow down!*

Twisting the arm, she snapped it off at the shoulder. Without hesitating, the knight swiveled and knocked Brodie's feet from under her. She hit the ground hard, and then his metal hand was on her throat.

Kicking at him, she tried to free herself, but his grip grew tighter.

Got to break free or I'm dead—

Grabbing the knight's fingers, she slowly pulled them apart, kicking at his shoulder joint. The remaining arm came loose and went limp. Struggling for breath, Brodie stumbled to her feet and tried to run, but now the knight took a mighty leap into the air. She turned as he came down, smashing her into the dirt.

Then his legs were around her throat, squeezing tightly.

This is ridiculous, she thought. *It can't end*

this way! Choked to death by a headless and armless knight!

Slamming her feet into his groin gained her another inch. She was able to breathe, but only just. She stood, lifting the knight into the air. Running towards a nearby house, she slammed his torso into a wall. The legs loosened. She did it again. And again.

Finally a leg came loose, and went clattering to the ground. Brodie gripped the remaining leg and swung the torso at the side of the house. It slammed into the wall and the leg came loose.

Brodie dropped to her knees, trying to breathe.

'I've been in some weird fights,' she said. 'But that's the strangest.'

Leaving the scattered pieces of the knight, she stumbled towards a nearby forest. Her foot still hurt, but she ignored the pain. A sound came from behind. One of the pieces of the knight—the head—was moving across the ground, as if drawn by an invisible thread.

'You've got to be kidding,' Brodie groaned.

The head clanked back onto the neck of the

knight. Next an arm started towards the torso, but Brodie had already seen enough.

Racing towards the forest, she reached it, breathing hard. A path led into the undergrowth. Only now did she have time to wonder how the knight could still be functioning. Without a head, or limbs, it had almost killed her. She might not be so lucky next time.

Stopping at a stream, she hungrily gulped down some water. There was no bird song in the forest. No chirruping of insects in the undergrowth. Only a terrible dead silence as if the whole world were caught in a single instant.

There's got to be a way out of here, she thought. Her time with the others had taught her to never give up. She would find a way out—or die trying.

Thud.

Something crashed in the forest behind her.

Thud.

Something was coming.

Something gigantic.

Chapter Twenty

The sound of laughter finished the instant Chad entered the room. He had been ready to smash anything that moved, but Ebony's bedroom had looked identical to how she had left it: neat, clean— and empty.

Turning back to Brodie, he saw the hallway was also empty.

'Brodie?'

No, he thought. *Not again!*

He charged from the room, but she was nowhere to be seen.

'No!' he cried. 'Not you too!'

The silence of the house closed around him like a shroud. He suddenly felt very afraid. First Ebony, then Dan and now Brodie were gone. Whisked away as if they'd never existed. At any moment—no—at any *second*, the same could happen to him.

This would be like the Marie Celeste, he thought. The ship had been found abandoned in the nineteenth century with its entire crew missing. There was never any explanation as to their fate. *If I disappear, no-one will ever know what happened to us.*

Chad felt weak at the knees. Everything had gone wrong from the moment they'd stepped into this house. *It's this house*, he thought. *I've got to get away from it and get help.* And there was really only one option.

Axel.

They may have had their ups and downs, but he knew Axel would sacrifice his own life to save any of them. Chad stared at the window at the other end of the hall. This wasn't the time to be discrete. Creating a block of ice, he threw it through the window, destroying it. Then he ran down the hall, creating a fireboard of super heated air beneath him, and flew out.

He wasn't an expert at flying, but that wasn't going to stop him now.

I've got to get to Axel, he thought. *Between the two of us, we can save the others. I'm sure we can!*

Chad flew away from the house, over the forest. It would take a few hours to reach Axel. He would do his best to not be seen while in flight, but there were so many superheroes flying around these days that the government—and The Agency—couldn't monitor them all.

A rumble rolled across the landscape. *What is that?* It sounded like an earthquake. Trees and dirt exploded from the forest ahead as a long black barrier, made of shining metal, rose from the ground. It stretched out to meet other walls rising up around the town.

Targo was being surrounded on all sides.

Chad cried out in amazement. The walls were rising so quickly that he would have to be fast to get over the top. He focused again on the fireboard of heated air beneath him, urging it to rise as he watched the top of the nearest wall.

This is crazy, he thought. *How can this be happening?*

Eight walls were forming an octagon around the town. As the walls rose higher and higher, Chad struggled to keep pace, focusing on urging more power to his fireboard. The wall ahead was five hundred feet high. Then a thousand. Shivering, Chad urged himself to fly faster. It was freezing up here, and getting colder by the second.

Still, the walls continued to climb.

This is impossible. Walls can't grow out of the earth. It doesn't make any sense.

He glanced downwards and immediately wished he hadn't. The landscape looked tiny, like a map. He tried concentrating on the wall ahead, but he couldn't help but think about how high he was above the ground. Falling from here would turn him into a splat on the ground.

Doubling his effort, he strove to climb higher, but the cold felt like it was leeching through his bones. The wind had built up to a gale. There was no way the wall could still be climbing. There was no way it could even *exist*, but still it continued to grow.

Chad felt tears in his eyes. He couldn't reach it. The wall was still rising. Now it was high above the clouds. He gave his fireboard one final push.

Veering close to the wall, he looked for a place to grab hold, but it was smooth. If he could hang on for a minute he could—

Slam!

He had not reached the wall, but had instead hit an invisible barrier that had sent him flying. He fell, head over heel.

I've got to survive this, he thought. *Got to save the others.*

Falling at terminal velocity, he would hit the ground within seconds. Spreading his arms and legs, he forced himself to sail on the wind, face down. It was terrifying, staring at the approaching landscape. Focusing on the spot under his body, he created a flame that grew increasingly hotter. Then he created a cold barrier above it.

The ground was frighteningly close—only a few hundred feet—but he concentrated on increasing the board's heat. His descent was slowing, but not fast enough. With one mighty burst of heat, he gave power to the white hot fireboard, slowing his descent with one last almighty burst.

Chad was thirty feet above the tree tops. Another second and he would have smashed into them. His legs were shaking uncontrollably. Forcing himself to control the fireboard, he coasted to the ground and tumbled off, sucking in mouthfuls of air. Grass pressed against his face.

He wept.

This was beyond anything he could ever have imagined. He wasn't *The Chad*. He was a stupid kid thinking he was a superhero. How could he ever believe he could save Ebony, Dan and Brodie?

He rolled over. The wall, fifty feet away, stretched thousands of feet into the air, piercing the clouds. *How is this possible?* Chad felt like he had wandered into a fairy land. Ever since they had landed in this town, it had felt like the laws of physics had gone south.

The whole town must be in a panic. Hell, the whole *world* must be wondering what was going on in Targo. The police would arrive. Then the Department of Defense. Superheroes and authorities would be here within hours.

Maybe he couldn't get out, but they could certainly get in.

A distant cry broke through his thoughts. He slowly sat up. It was a voice. A familiar voice. Struggling to his feet, he scrambled over vegetation until he met a path. He followed it.

Oh no.

He was back at the Cooper house. Ebony's voice was coming from the house. His legs shaking, Chad climbed the front steps and entered.

No, no, no.

He could hear Ebony screaming.

Dry mouthed, he staggered into the dining room. The voice was louder now. She was screaming as if in terrible pain.

'Ebony!' he yelled. 'Where are you?'

The sound stopped.

Clenching his fists, he swung about in fury. The powers that controlled this house—this town— were playing with him. 'Where is my sister?' he yelled. 'Where are Brodie and Dan? What have you done with them?'

Silence.

'I'll tear this house apart!' he snapped. 'I'll burn this town to the ground searching for them! I'll make you pay—'

Chad stopped. His mouth fell open in astonishment as he fell to his knees.

No, he thought. *It's not possible.*

But he could see it with his own eyes. The dining room was unchanged from the first time he had entered it, except for one of the paintings. The painting of the castle was unchanged, as were the ones of the ship at sea and the fox hunt.

But the one of green fields near a forest had three tiny figures in it—Brodie, Dan and Ebony. A giant creature, a hundred feet tall, was chasing them and would crush them in seconds.

Chapter Twenty-One

So, I thought. *This is my room.*

The house in Kansas where I grew up had been sold and most of the possessions packed up or given away. My belongings had been brought here. A few things had been taken out to make the room more homely, but most remained in cardboard boxes.

I turned slowly, trying to take in every detail in a single glance.

On the table next to my bed was a lava lamp. I'd never taken any particular interest in them, but obviously my pre-Axel self did. And that was going to take some getting used to as well. My name was Adam. Axel was gone.

Boy, this really was a whole new life.

Henry and Louise have already put up some of my old posters. A band called *Singing Lizards*, another called *Fire Head* as well as some really old bands—*Kiss* and *ACDC*. I didn't know I had such a taste in music.

Slowly, I unpacked the boxes. There were clothes. Most of them looked too small. I'd obviously grown a lot over the last year. The books looked a lot more appealing. A lot of adventure, dystopian fiction and sci-fi. I must have had an interest in outer space long before I got there.

Turning the pages, I saw plenty of dog-eared corners, a habit I did not have in my new life. There was something about the turned over corners that worried me, but I had no idea what.

The games were what you'd expect— Monopoly, Clue and a few one hit wonders that didn't make it past the summer. Opening the Monopoly game, I study the board and the pieces for a moment. My parents and I played this board, sat around it and shared valuable hours together.

Gripping the pieces in my hands, I try to evoke a sense of them, a feel for my past life, but I drew a blank. If anything, I felt a sense of disquiet as I studied the pieces.

Why?

I had no idea.

My bedroom was at the rear of the house, overlooking open fields. Henry and Louise were both retired. They'd been potato farmers. A downturn in the market, and the deaths of my parents, had finally made them decide to sell their farm and move to Ohio.

A knock came at the door.

'Adam?' Henry said, sticking his head though. 'How're you settling in?'

'Fine,' I said, although nothing could be further from the truth. 'Just taking a look around.'

'You can do more than that,' Henry said, smiling. 'This is your home.'

That was going to take some getting used to.

'Would you like a tour of the place?'

'Sure.'

Henry explained the property had previously been used to grow hay for livestock. The owner had lost money in the stock market and sold off acreage to cover his debt. The remaining section with the house was too small to produce any sizable crops.

'We're thinking about doing some market gardening,' Henry said, as we strolled across a grassy field. 'Nothing too big. Tomatoes, carrots, potatoes. A variety of things.'

Living in Ohio would be strange after everything I'd been through over the last few months.

Henry seemed to read my mind. 'We know about your escapades,' he said. 'Or some of them, anyway.'

'Like what?'

He shrugged. 'The less said, the better.' Walking in silence, we followed a path around the property. 'Though it doesn't look like you need ever worry about paying for flights.'

I laughed. 'Not really,' I said. 'I can probably give you a ride if you like.'

Now he laughed. 'I don't even go up in planes,' he said.

'Flying's still the safest way to travel.'

'I'll take your word for it.' Henry grew serious. 'I thought your aunt was crazy when she recognized you in that newspaper picture. She insisted on visiting that alien city, almost forced her way in to talk to those aliens.'

'Tomay and Bax.'

Henry nodded. 'Those government types wanted to question her first,' he said. 'But Louise wouldn't open her mouth. We don't get involved in politics. We don't care what you've done, or what you've been involved in, we just wanted you here with us.

'She finally got in and spoke to those aliens. She was scared, but she did it. I still thought she was crazy. I was sure you'd been killed in that accident with your parents.'

'Somehow I must have survived,' I mused. How did The Agency find me? Did they arrange the accident? Did they kill my parents so they could use me for their experiments?

'That's how much Louise wanted you home,' Henry continued. 'Now there's something I want to say to you. Louise, your aunt, is still broken up about losing her sister and your dad. It affected her very badly. It might be best if you don't ask too much about them.'

'Okay.' This was a shame because I wanted to ask her *everything* about them. 'I'll watch what I say.'

The ground was dry. We were coming into summer and Henry thought it would be a hot one. He talked about planting crops, but my mind was a million miles away with Brodie and the others. What were they doing now?

We returned to the house, where Henry showed me through. We lingered in Louise's painting room. She specialized in landscapes, scenes of farmhouses in lonely fields and sunrises over haystacks. I felt another twinge of disquiet, but I didn't know why.

'We've got a surprise visitor arriving this afternoon,' Henry said.

'Who is it?'

'It wouldn't be a surprise if I told you.' Henry was smiling, but he reddened. 'It was Louise's idea.'

He looked kind of embarrassed and wouldn't say more. He turned the radio on in the kitchen and the twangs of country music drifted through the home. I went to my bedroom and read for a while. In the back of my mind, I kept wondering about the surprise. There had been surprises in the past—aliens, monsters and super villains. Whatever this was probably wasn't in the same realm.

At some point in the afternoon, I fell asleep, awaking a few hours later with my book plastered to my face. Wondering what had woken me, I heard the sound of an engine cutting out. It looked like Louise was home.

Before I had a chance to climb out of bed, she appeared in the doorway. 'Wake up, sleepyhead,' she said. 'There's someone who wants to see you.'

'Who is it?'

'You'll see.' Louise lowered her voice. 'She doesn't know about your...you know.'

My powers.

Louise led me into the kitchen where Henry stood, making a coffee. Next to him stood a pixie-faced girl with red hair, a duffle bag at her side. Her face lighting up with excitement, she ran over and gave me a huge hug.

'I didn't believe it,' she said, tears in her eyes. 'Your aunt told me she found you, but I thought she was mistaken.'

I stared at her in complete confusion.

'You really don't know how I am?' the girl said, her face falling.

'I'm sorry. I don't remember—'

'I'm Quinn,' she said. 'I'm your girlfriend.'

Chapter Twenty-Two

I stared at her for what seemed like an eternity.

'Did you hear me?' she asked. 'I'm Quinn. I'm—'

'I heard you.'

Possibly the most disturbing part of this wasn't her revelation that she was my girlfriend. It was that she looked so much like Brodie. Her hair was identical, face a similar shape and she had the same athletic body. It was like looking at Brodie through a fractured lens.

I glanced over at Louise whose smile had faded to dismay. 'I'm sorry,' she said, nervously. 'I thought it would be a pleasant surprise. That was foolish of me.'

'Pleasant?' I felt sick. 'I feel like I'm in some kind of...freak show!'

Storming from the house, I somehow stopped myself from flying off into the sunset. That's what I felt like doing. Flying away and never coming back. In frustration, I made for a hill further up the road.

After a few minutes, I heard footsteps behind me as someone kept pace.

'I've never had that reaction before,' Quinn's voice said from behind. 'Usually boys are pleased to see me.'

My mind was such a jumble of emotions I couldn't speak. A lump in my throat seemed so big it was ready to choke me. The road petered away, giving way to long grass as I started up the hill. Storming through it, I was breathing heavily by the time I reached the top. This was the highest ground for miles. Fields and wooded areas spread out on all sides. A town—presumably Halliford—lay a few miles to the north.

I wiped sweat away from my brow as a cool breeze pulled at my hair. Once again I wanted to fly away, but if I did that I might never be able to return. Quinn could know everything about my superhero past, or nothing at all. I couldn't risk blowing my cover before I'd even settled into this new life.

Quinn finally reached me. 'Can you say something?' she said. 'I'm all out of words.'

An apology was in order. 'I'm sorry I reacted like that,' I said. 'It was a shock.'

'Louise should have told you,' Quinn said, looking out at the view. 'She thought seeing me like that might trigger some memories.' Her eyes met mine. 'Did it?'

Memories? No. What it was now triggering was the terrible realization that maybe the only reason I'd been in a relationship with Brodie was because of her resemblance to Quinn. Maybe my amnesia riddled brain had transferred my affections from one girl to the other.

Had I ever been in love with Brodie? Or had I simply replaced Quinn for her?

'I don't remember you at all,' I said. 'I wish I did.'

Her face fell. 'I know this must be really hard for you,' Quinn said. 'It is for me too.'

We were almost face-to-face. I shot a look at her. She was attractive, but I could see tears at the corner of her eyes.

'Can you understand what it's like for me?'

she asked. 'I thought you were dead, washed away with your parents, and drowned. I went to a memorial service for you. I prayed over a grave with no body in it. You think that's easy?'

I hadn't really thought about this. My parents were buried somewhere. There was a memorial marker with my name on it too. Technically, I was both alive and dead at the same time. But that wasn't the issue right now. People had mourned my loss. One of them was Quinn. It was strange to think of her crying her eyes out after losing me, and I didn't remember her at all.

'I'm sorry,' I said. 'This is more difficult than I expected.'

'It's not easy for me either. I came here because Louise told me I had to come. She said it was a matter of life and death.'

'She didn't tell you about me?'

'She couldn't, otherwise the authorities would know and for some reason she wants to keep you quiet.' Quinn frowned. 'Anyway, I only found out an hour ago you were alive.'

'Have you...moved on?'

'Moved on? You make it sound like changing houses.'

'I mean—'

'I know what you mean.' Quinn pouted, again eerily reminiscent of Brodie. 'The answer is no.'

'No?'

'No, I don't have a boyfriend.'

We stared out across the open fields. A farmer in the distance was driving a harvester, throwing dust and brown grass into the air. A hawk flew overhead, dived towards something in a field and scooped it up. I watched until the bird was only a dot in the distance, and then nothing.

'We should head back to the house,' I said.

Quinn nodded.

Traipsing down the hill, I saw Louise and Henry's home. My home. Henry was at the side of the house, shading his eyes from the sun, watching us. He gave a single wave and I waved back.

These people aren't my enemies, I thought. *So why am I treating them like they are?*

'How long are you staying?' I asked.

'I'm not sure. A week. Maybe more. I've got to get back to school soon.'

School. That's right. Some kids still did that.

'I'm staying at your place,' Quinn continued. 'Hopefully we can hang out.'

'Of course we will.'

Quinn pursed her lips. 'There's still something I've got to know,' she said, hesitantly. 'Louise explained about your amnesia and how you were taken in by some family. But, well, were you with someone else?'

'There was someone,' I said, slowly, 'but that's over now.'

'What was her name?'

'Brodie.'

'Are you sure it's over? Completely?'

'One hundred percent.'

We walked through the gates of the farm. The smell of cooking food wafted from the house. It smelt like stewing meat. Climbing the front steps, I looked out across the fields. The sun was low in the sky.

Another day was drawing to a close. In the last couple of days I had lost one family and gained another.

We stopped at the door.

'You know,' Quinn said. 'I'm not sure that love ever dies.'

'I said that was all over with Brodie.'

Quinn's eyes met mine. 'I wasn't talking about Brodie.'

Chapter Twenty-Three

'Adam?' The voice came from a million miles away. 'Wake up.'

I blearily opened my eyes. *Who is Adam?* I wondered. Then I remembered. *I'm Adam.* The overhead light in my room was off, but my bedside lamp showed Louise, dressed in pajamas and a dressing gown. Glancing at the clock, I saw it was just after midnight.

'What's wrong?' I asked.

'There's been an accident,' she said. 'On the interstate about ten miles from here.'

'Oh?' I sat up, rubbing my eyes. 'What happened?'

'It was on the radio. There was a bad fog. A petrol tanker jackknifed. There's a fire. The fire department's trying to put it out, but it's chaos over there.'

'Why are you telling me this?'

'At first I didn't think anything of it,' Louise said, her face haunted. 'But then I thought about you and your powers. The things you can do.'

'That's finished now.'

She nodded. 'That's what I thought too,' she said. 'But isn't it wrong to let someone needlessly suffer?'

I couldn't argue with that. 'But if I'm seen—'

'Get your clothing on,' she said. 'I've got a covering for your head.'

Within minutes, I was dressed and Louise had found a balaclava for me to wear. I thought it made me look like a bank robber. Reaching the back porch, I saw a red glow on the horizon.

'That looks bad,' I said.

'Be careful,' Louise said, grabbing my arm. 'If anything were to happen to you—'

'I'll be fine.'

I leapt into the night. The air was full of smoke and fuel, even from this distance. Putting on a burst of speed, I was over the accident in minutes. It wasn't hard to work out how it happened. The fog had reduced visibility to only a few feet. A car had clipped a petrol tanker coming in the opposite direction. The tanker had slid onto its side. It hadn't exploded, but another vehicle was on fire with a dozen others in a multi-car pileup. An ambulance was there, but the fire brigade were nowhere to be seen.

I landed next to an ambulance driver working on a patient on the road. It looked bad.

'Where's the fire brigade?' I asked.

The man looked at me in astonishment for a second. Recovering, he said, 'There's a big fire over in Tyson,' he said. 'A dozen brigades. They're trying to get an engine over here, but—'

Ka-boom!

There was a flash of light, followed by a wall of heat. I threw up a barrier as the petrol tanker exploded and the blast hit us. Protecting the driver and his patient from the worst of it, I used my powers to divert the path of the shrapnel. If I'd been an instant slower, the debris would have sliced us to pieces.

The explosion had thrown a dozen vehicles about like toys. Flames a hundred feet high were shooting into the air. Smoke was everywhere. I bent close to the ambulance driver.

'Can you move him?' I asked.

'We'll have to.'

Using my powers to levitate the three of us into the air, I floated us a few hundred feet away and settled them onto the ground. The driver continued to work on his patient as I flew back to the heart of the devastation. The remains of the tanker were burning out of control. Fortunately, fire needed air to breathe.

Flying straight up, I focused on removing all the air from the scene of the blast. Within a minute, the blaze was extinguished, although there were still spot fires around the cars. Turning my attention to the victims, I immediately found a person trapped under a vehicle. Lifting the car away, I discovered he was already beyond help.

I should have been faster, I thought.

But I had to push the tragedy from my mind. I began searching the other vehicles. A woman had taken refuge on the floor of her car. I used my powers to expand the air between the doors hinges, and pulled it off. She ran for her life. A family of three had also taken refuge. The father had broken his arm in the blast. Once again, the doors were jammed shut, so I broke them off, allowing them to escape.

I wished Brodie and the team were here. Many hands really do make light work. A police car arrived, and the officers leapt into action, and soon after, another ambulance. The paramedics started lifting someone free from a damaged car.

Reaching a wrecked vehicle, I found a woman not moving. I checked her pulse. No breath either. Easing her onto the road, I started CPR, compressing her chest, breathing into her mouth to force the most vital of necessity of life—air—into her lungs. Checking her pulse again, I found nothing, but I persevered.

Another minute passed. Ready to give up, I was surprised to notice her face had regained some of its color.

Keep going, I told myself.

Back at The Agency, a time that seemed a million years in the past, we had all been trained in first aid. I knew life could be restored if oxygen and blood flow were restored in time. After that, brain damage and, finally, death would occur.

By now, sweat was pouring off me. CPR was tough business. I wasn't sure how long I could keep this up.

The woman coughed, her eyes fluttering open.

'Where...what happened?' she groaned.

'There was an accident,' I said. 'A tanker exploded.'

'Who are you?'

I realized I was still wearing the balaclava. 'A friend,' I said. 'You were in a bad way.'

More ambulances were arriving. Fire engines were finally on the scene. An ambulance woman knelt next to me, giving me an odd look.

'Are you injured?' she asked.

'No, I was just passing by.' She was staring at my disguise. 'I don't always dress like this.'

'I'm sure.'

I leapt into the sky, leaving her and the chaos behind. In seconds I was among the clouds. I had missed this, the freedom of flight.

How could I ever give this up?

For the next hour I coasted over the countryside, watching the dark world beneath. The fires were soon extinguished and the emergency vehicles headed off into the night. Soon I was floating above the earth, not asleep, not awake.

Finally I flew back towards the farm. It wasn't hard to find. Every other property was in darkness. Ours was the only home with a light on the back porch. Gliding into land, I found Louise on the step. She raced over and hugged me tight.

'I was worried,' she said.

'I'm okay.' We went into the kitchen. The house was quiet after the chaos on the road. 'I just needed some time to think.'

'Were you all right with helping out?'

'Of course,' I said. 'Why wouldn't I be?'

Louise nodded thoughtfully. 'I thought you would be,' she said. 'I'm glad you are.'

I peered at her, curiously. 'Why? What do you mean?'

'Now isn't the time to talk,' she said. 'We'll speak in the morning.'

I pressed her, but she wouldn't say anything more. Climbing into bed, I expected to stay awake, but I was asleep within seconds.

Chapter Twenty-Four

I awoke to the rattle of running water.

Blinking, I climbed out of bed. Someone was showering. A radio played an old country song. The smell of cooked food wafted through the house. Making my way to the kitchen, I found Louise making bacon and eggs.

'You're up,' she said, smiling. 'I'm glad you slept in.'

'Who's in the bathroom?' I asked.

'Quinn. Henry's gone into Halliford to buy supplies.'

Scratching my head and yawning, I offered to help, but Louise waved me away. 'I've made breakfast a million times,' she said. 'It'll only take a minute.'

Settling into the breakfast nook, I looked through the window at the fields beyond. The day before, I had thought them uninviting. Now, after helping out the previous night, I wondered if there might be a way I could have the best of both worlds.

'What did you mean last night?' I asked

Louise. 'When you said about me helping out?'

She dished food onto a plate. 'We won't talk yet,' she said. 'Henry's due back soon. He's taking Quinn into town so she can buy some clothing. She came over here so quickly she didn't bring much of a wardrobe.' Pouring coffee, Louise sat down. 'We'll go into town with them. There's a nice cafe where we can chat.'

By the time I finished breakfast, Quinn was washed and dressed. She looked nice, dressed in a blue and white striped dress, reminiscent of Dorothy from Wizard of Oz. Henry arrived home, and we all piled into the car with him.

Sitting in the back seat with Quinn, I realized I didn't know what to say to her. I barely knew Quinn. Henry put on the radio and an old Johnny Cash song played. As the truck rattled down a rough road, Quinn bumped into me.

'Sorry,' she murmured.

I smiled, not knowing what to say. 'Your hair looks nice,' I said.

'It's the same as yesterday.'

'But you've washed it,' I said. 'Yesterday it had bugs and trash in it.'

'You've still got the same sense of humor. Some things never change.'

If you say so, I thought.

Halliford was busy, but not huge. It had a couple of supermarkets and several dozen specialty stores. Passing the local high school, I realized I might go there one day. A big baseball game was coming up. It made me wonder if I'd played baseball or football.

'You were okay at both,' Quinn said, when I asked her. 'A master of none.'

'Is that like saying I was terrible?'

She laughed. 'Not too terrible.'

Henry stopped in the heart of town and dropped Louise and me off at a cafe called *The Tender Rose*.

'Very fragrant,' I joked.

Louise smiled. Henry drove off, promising to return in an hour. Quinn waved, looking a little sad. I began to understand what it was like for her. She'd lost me—the boy she loved—just as I'd lost my memory. The losses were painful for us both.

Settling into a booth, Louise ordered an early lunch—homemade lasagne—for both of us.

Without any preamble, Louise asked me again how I felt about helping the people at the tanker crash.

'It felt good,' I said. 'Why are you asking me? What are you trying to get at?'

'I haven't been completely honest with you,' Louise said. 'Oh, I haven't lied. I wouldn't do that, but there is something I should mention.'

I waited.

'It wasn't me that identified you from that picture,' Louise continued. 'It was someone else. A man who came to see us. His name was Cameron Howard.'

'Okay,' I said, unsure.

'He said he worked for an organization called Rescue Prime, an international rescue group.'

'I've never heard of them.'

'They're not a part of any government, so

they're not very well known. There was a major problem on the International Space Station last year. The entire crew was almost killed, but Rescue Prime saved them.'

'Really?' I hadn't heard anything about this. 'There was nothing in the media about it.'

'Governments don't advertise when things go wrong. They pay a fee to belong to Rescue Prime to keep things quiet.'

'Who—exactly—is Rescue Prime?'

'They're modified humans like you. Apparently they've saved over a million lives in the last decade alone.'

I was open-mouthed. 'That's amazing,' I said. 'And they want me to join?'

Louise nodded.

I sat there in stunned silence. This had all come out of nowhere. Rescue Prime. A covert organization. Cameron Howard.

'But what about...well, I had some problems with The Agency...'

'That'll all be forgotten. They have no

affiliation with The Agency. It means you could live here with us and still be part of a good cause.'

Our food arrived and I ate in thoughtful silence. This was amazing. Flying over the darkened landscape the previous night, I had realized living on the farm wasn't going to cut it. I had moved beyond harvesting crops. Maybe even beyond school and everything that a normal life offered.

But to have the best of both worlds...

'Maybe we could get Brodie and the others onboard too,' I said. 'Didn't they ask about them?'

'They didn't mention anyone else from *Liber8tor*,' Louise said. 'Maybe you can speak to this Cameron Howard guy about them. That is,' she added, 'if you want to meet him.'

Nodding slowly, I said, 'I do.'

The door to the cafe opened and Quinn appeared. It was a good thing I had finished eating, because my mouth fell open in amazement. Quinn had not only bought a new outfit—a skin-tight floral dress with a pair of matching shoes—she'd also had her hair styled. She looked a million dollars.

'You look incredible,' I said.

'Thank you,' she said, giving a small curtsey.

We climbed back into the truck and headed back to the farm. On the way, I glanced over at Quinn, telling her again how fantastic she looked. She just smiled and blushed. Reaching the farm, we went to the back veranda and settled into the swing chair to look at the view. It was a beautiful afternoon, the kind you'd wish would last forever. We made small talk for a while.

Without warning, she leant over and kissed me. Hard. We spent about ten minutes making out before she pushed her hair back and apologized.

'I'm not usually like that,' she said. 'But I've missed you.'

I took her hand. 'It must have been really hard for you,' I said. 'I'm sorry.'

'You don't need to be sorry.'

'But I am. It's going to take me a while to get back to who I was.'

'I understand.'

I stood, staring out at the endless landscape.

'I'm going for a walk,' I said. 'I need to think about a few things.'

'I've got work to do,' Quinn said, smiling. 'Lots of new dresses to try on.'

Strolling away from the building, I took a deep breath and gazed into the distance. This was all so perfect.

What a shame it was all a complete lie.

Chapter Twenty-Five

The house was just right. Louise and Henry were the ideal aunt and uncle. They looked like a typical farmer and his wife, a couple who had spent their lives working the land. Their explanation of the accident was logical: my parents had been killed, but I had been saved, taken in by The Agency and modified.

Quinn was the clincher. She was the sort of girl a guy could settle down with for the rest of his life.

It was all so perfect.

Too perfect.

There was no way Louise could have known we christened our ship *Liber8tor*. Outside of our group, no-one else knew its name. Yet, back at the cafe, she had said, '*They didn't mention anyone else from Liber8tor.*'

How did she know the name of our ship? She could only know it if someone else had told her. I know I didn't, and neither did Brodie. This guy, Cameron Howard, couldn't have known either. So how did they find out? Was *Liber8tor* bugged or—?

The answer hit me in a flash.

Back at New Haven, I had referred to our ship as *Liber8tor*. The information must have been relayed to Louise—or whatever her real name was.

Were Tomay and Bax in on this? Probably not. More than likely, they were innocent victims of this whole scam. They had simply made the mistake of trusting Louise when she'd turned up on their doorstep, pretending to be searching for her long lost nephew. Their residence must be bugged by whoever was behind this.

My stomach turned over. How long had this been in the planning? What was their ultimate goal? And what had happened to the others?

I had reached the halfway point of my walk. The house was still in view. I would reach it in about fifteen minutes. Slowing my pace, I pretended to soak up the sun as I continued around the perimeter.

This whole thing wasn't a ploy to capture us. Or kill us. That much was obvious. They could have done that already. We had fallen so completely for their story that they could have murdered us a dozen times over. Part of their plan was to get me to work for Rescue Prime, or whatever they called themselves. Were they a rescue organization? Probably not. More than likely, they were a group of mercenaries.

Where were Brodie, Chad and the others? Had they been captured by Cameron Howard? Were they even alive?

Passing behind a tree, out of sight of the house, I tried my comm bracelet. No reply came back. It could mean a poor signal, but I doubted it. *Liber8tor* had either been destroyed, captured or incapacitated. Most likely Brodie and the others were being held, or tricked, as I had been.

They had to be alive. All this hadn't been done simply to trap me. Their plan was to capture and use us all. How could I find the others? I couldn't simply confront Quinn and my faux family. They would clam up. If I threatened them, they wouldn't believe I'd torture them for information. I never had before, so I was unlikely to start now.

I needed to pretend everything was fine until I found out where my friends were being held.

Now, as I circled back to the house, I saw Quinn appear at a window. She waved. Smiling, I returned the greeting, though I wanted to smash her face in.

Choosing someone who resembled Brodie was a nice touch. Obviously they'd assumed I would simply transfer my affection to her. They didn't understand the human heart too well.

Reaching the house, I went to my bedroom. Even if I could contact the others, it was undoubtedly not safe to talk here. Pottering about my room for the next half hour, I moved and rearranged things, put posters up on the walls and unpacked clothing. Turning over a lamp, I found a small black button at the base. A microphone. I was bugged. Probably the entire house was one big surveillance operation.

Wait a minute...

I glanced down at the watch Louise had given me. She's said this was from my old life, but I would have bet money it contained a tracking and recording device. Climbing onto my bed, I lay back, trying to appear relaxed, although inside I was shaking, scared and angry.

It seemed I had nothing on my side, but that wasn't true. I knew this whole escapade was one huge lie, and I could use that to my advantage.

Later in the day, as Louise and Quinn cooked dinner, I played chess with Henry. He was a good player. I'll give him that. He didn't let me win. We traded verbal blows through the game.

'You've left your knight undefended,' Henry said, raising an eyebrow.

'All part of my cunning plan,' I said, laughing evilly. 'Soon you will regret your attacking posture.'

In the end, he didn't regret anything. He caught me in checkmate while I still had most of my pieces on the board. We played a second game, but I fared even worse.

'Chess takes patience and concentration,' Henry advised. 'An even mixture of both.'

'I'll keep that in mind.'

Dinner and dessert followed soon after.

Louise knew how to make a mean cheesecake. As we dived in, Quinn mentioned how much she was loving the area, and hated the idea of leaving.

'We'd love you to stay,' Louise said, giving her hand a squeeze. 'It's wonderful having another girl around.'

'My parents have me on a pretty loose leash,' Quinn said. 'They're not in a big hurry to have me back.'

'What about school?'

'Actually,' Quinn looked embarrassed, 'my parents have been talking about splitting up.'

'I'm sorry to hear that.'

Quinn glanced over at me. Clearly, this was all staged for my benefit, the idea being that she would eventually stay here permanently. One day we would be married. Oh, what a happy family we would be.

I resisted the urge to puke.

Chapter Twenty-Six

After a couple of hours of TV, where I sat with my arm draped around Quinn's shoulder, I gave a few obvious yawns and said I was turning in. The family wished me goodnight before I disappeared to my room.

I spent the next three hours lying in bed, completely awake. I couldn't have slept if I'd been paid. Sometime after one, I heard the creak of floorboards as a person left the house. Removing my watch, I left it on my bedside table, eased the window open and climbed out.

Quinn got into her car and drove off. Taking to the skies, I followed. The air was cool as I trailed her, watching the headlights cut through the dark like a pair of knives. It was a dark night, the crescent moon shouldered behind clouds. She drove west for almost an hour, reaching an industrial building on the far side of Halliford.

Wilson Electrics.

It looked like the place had been abandoned for years. She drove through the front gates and parked. Producing a flashlight, she flashed it at the building, sending a signal. A figure broke from the darkness. I floated down to hide behind some old pallets as the two figures came together.

Quinn started speaking.

Slam!

The man had punched her in the stomach—hard. He said something more to her as she struggled back to her feet, but I couldn't make it out. They spoke for another few minutes. Then Quinn limped away back to the car, climbed in and drove off.

I wasn't sure what to make of all this. There was obviously a dispute going on between Quinn and the man. She was obviously not an equal partner in this whole thing. Although I longed to search the old factory, I realized Quinn would be back home within minutes. If I was found gone from my bed, the game would be up.

Taking to the skies again, I flew home and went to sleep.

The next morning at breakfast, I saw the first break in their facade. Louise and Henry were true to character, but Quinn looked miserable. She gave me a smile, but looked ready to burst into tears. I took her outside as soon as I could to speak.

'I'm fine,' she said, wiping away a tear. 'I'm just upset that we've wasted so much time being apart.'

Another lie.

'Let's go out,' I said.

'Where?'

'Somewhere.'

Leaving the house, we walked to the hill we had climbed a few days previous. Quinn chatted, but I could tell she was distracted. Reaching the top, we looked out at the view. A bank of gray clouds clotted the horizon. As Quinn took my hand, I drew her close and looked into her eyes.

'What did you want to talk about?' Quinn asked.

'You and me,' I said. 'But mostly how you're going to be sorry if you don't tell me the truth.'

I took off, hugging Quinn tightly against me. She screamed. Within seconds we were hundreds of feet above the ground. Quinn struggled, trying to claw at my face. Then she reached for a locket around her neck.

'Is that a communicator?' I said. 'I wouldn't touch that if I were you.'

By now we were a mile up where the air was cold and clear.

'Why?' she snapped, furious tears in her eyes. 'You're not going to—'

I dropped her. It's frightening how fast a person falls when they're a mile off the ground. There's this thing called terminal velocity. It's the maximum speed you can travel at. Here on Earth, it's about 120 miles per hour. That's how fast skydivers fall.

Skydiving can be scary if you haven't done it before. Imagine doing it without a parachute.

I grabbed Quinn in midair about a hundred feet before she struck the ground. She was utterly terrified, but not so frightened that she wasn't still fighting me.

'Put me down!' she yelled, as we ascended

again.

'Sure.'

So I dropped her again.

This time when I caught her, she looked positively ill.

'Why are you doing this?' she demanded. 'I haven't done anything to you.'

I gripped her collar. 'Really? Care to explain why you were meeting that guy at Wilson Electrics?

Quinn's chin quivered. 'I don't know what you're talking about.'

'Sure you do.'

'I can't tell you. People's lives are at risk.'

'Try me.'

She shook her head resolutely. 'You can drop me as many times as you want,' she said, 'but you won't kill me.'

'You're right,' I said. 'I'm not that sort of guy.' I stared into her eyes. 'But you'd better believe I'll take you somewhere so remote it'll be months before you find your way out again. Maybe the Amazon. Maybe Antarctica.'

'You...you can't mean that,' she said, her resolve finally faltering.

But I did mean it, and she could see it in my face.

'It's my father,' she said flatly. 'They've got him.'

I gently lowered us into a wooded area near the base of the hill.

'Who are they?'

'How much do you know?'

'I know this whole thing is a sham. That you're no more my girlfriend than Louise and Henry are my aunt and uncle.'

'I was recruited by Cameron Howard.'

'And Rescue Prime?'

'There is no Rescue Prime. Howard and his men were going to recruit you to help them break into a facility to steal a deadly virus.'

'I would never have done such a thing.'

'They were going to tell you it was an influenza cure. Do you know how many people the flu kills every year?'

About a million, I knew.

'What about Brodie and the others?' I asked.

'I don't know anything about them.'

'But why this subterfuge?'

'That was the deal. Howard got you in return for the others.'

I swallowed. 'Are they safe?' I asked. 'How do I find them?'

'I don't know.'

'You're lying.'

'I'm not.'

'Why were you recruited?' I asked. 'It wasn't because of your pretty face.'

'They're holding my father, Robert Okada,' she said. 'And it *was* because of my pretty face.'

Her face shuddered, and melted into that of Louise. Then Henry. And half a dozen famous movie stars. Quinn was a shape shifter. She could mimic other people with ease.

'What's your real name?' I asked.

'Quinn, believe it or not,' she said. 'My father once worked for The Agency. He had me modified, thinking it was for the best.'

'And was it?'

'Not really. I was always getting into trouble.' She sighed. 'A few months ago, my father was kidnapped. I was told I had to cooperate or he'd be killed.'

'Where is Cameron Howard?'

Quinn pursed her lips. 'I can't tell you,' she said. 'They'll kill my father.'

'Your father's in danger whatever you do. With my help, we can rescue your father and the others.'

Quinn thought for a long moment. 'All right,' she said, finally. 'I'll do as you say. But we've got to rescue my dad first. Then we can save your friends.'

I nodded. It wasn't what I wanted, but it was the best I could negotiate. I just hoped we weren't too late.

Chapter Twenty-Seven

Chad stared at the painting in horror. Brodie and the others were seconds away from death—and there was nothing he could do about it.

Or was there?

Staring at the picture, it looked more like a photo taken from high above the ground. Chad could even hear the roar of the beast. He shook his head. *I'm going mad*, he thought. *This can't be real.*

Real or not, he had to do something. With shaking hands, he reached up to the painting. His fingernails found the edge of the canvas. He dug them in and pulled. The canvas ripped...

...and air flowed through the gap.

This is crazy...

Pulling harder, he tore the canvas all the way back, revealing a gap overlooking the field where Dan and the others were being pursued. Chad gripped the edge of the frame and pulled himself through.

He fell. Sky was all about him, the landscape below. Creating a fireboard, he landed on it and peered down. The creature looked like a huge grizzly bear on two legs, but its mouth was a hole in its stomach, ringed with rows of sharp teeth. Grabbing Dan, the creature lifted him towards the hole.

Chad shot a blast of fire at the creature's head. Screaming in pain and fury, it dropped Dan and swatted at Chad. Flying in low, Chad veered clear of its clawed hand and caught Dan in midair.

'Where'd you come from?' Dan asked, amazed.

'Never mind that,' Chad said. 'Let's get the others.'

Settling Dan down, Chad fired a block of ice at the creature. It roared, knocking the projectile away. Charging towards them, it opened his mouth wide and a spike flew out.

'Watch out!' Dan yelled.

Chad deflected the spike with a block of ice.

That would have impaled us, he thought. *We've got to get out of here.*

He encased the creature in ice, but the huge block immediately began to crack. Brodie and Ebony raced to him, and Chad gave them a brief hug.

'Thank God you're okay,' he said. 'How did you end up here?'

'Never mind that now,' Brodie said. 'We need to get away.'

Chad formed a fireboard large enough for them all. The block of ice encasing the monster shattered. Shaking its body, it lurched towards them as Chad took off. Peering upwards, he saw the tiny window in the sky, a dark rectangle against the blue.

This is bizarre, he thought. *How can such a thing exist?*

They soared to the opening. First Ebony, then Brodie climbed into the gap.

Dan glared at him. 'This doesn't mean I forgive you for being a pain,' he said.

'No-one else has,' Chad grinned. 'Why should you?'

Dan disappeared through the hole, and Chad followed, allowing the board to evaporate. Tangled in a pile of arms and legs on the dining room floor, they watched as the frame of the painting cracked, broke and was dragged into the middle, as if by a whirlpool.

Ping!

It disappeared completely. Chad and the others clambered to their feet.

'This just gets weirder and weirder,' Ebony said.

'You've got to tell me exactly what happened,' Chad said. 'All of it.'

He listened for the next few minutes as they told their stories. Finally Brodie explained they had each raced from the forest at the same time, catching sight of each other. At that moment their powers had failed.

'What?' Chad said. 'Usually only a zeno emitter can do that.'

'It's true,' Brodie said. 'I even felt my strength evaporate, but I'm usually impervious to zeno rays.'

'What's going on?' Dan said. 'It's like we've fallen into some parallel dimension.'

'Well, it gets even stranger,' Chad said, telling them about the huge walls that surrounded Targo. 'I tried flying out, but they just grew higher and higher.

And Ferdy doesn't answer when I try contacting him.'

The others tried their comm bracelets, but also got static.

'I wish we'd never come here,' Dan said. 'It's a madhouse.'

'Maybe we can break through the wall if we all work together,' Brodie said.

They followed the trail through the forest to the wall, where great mounds of earth had been thrown up, and trees uprooted. Climbing over a shattered tree trunk, they reached the black divider. Dan gingerly tapped it.

'I wasn't able to touch it before,' Chad said.

'Well, it's safe now. I don't think it's made of metal, but it's not stone either.'

Dan tried manipulating it, Brodie tried hitting it, Chad tried melting it and Ebony tried to turn it into another substance. None of them had any success.

'It's as if our powers aren't working,' Brodie said.

Ebony turned a nearby rock into carbon. 'My

powers are working,' she said. 'But just not on the wall.'

'Everything's been weird since we arrived here,' Dan said.

'I wonder how the townsfolk are dealing with this,' Brodie said, turning to Chad. 'Have you seen any sign of the National Guard? Or the government?'

'No.'

'Let's go and find Mavis. I'd be interested to find out what she thinks.'

Chad and the others made their way back to Mavis's house. It was growing prematurely dark; the walls had cut off direct sunlight. Until they found a way out of here, the days would be four or five hours at most.

There was no answer at the old lady's door.

'I hope she's all right,' Ebony said.

'She may have gone into town,' Chad said. 'I'd do that if a huge unexplained wall went up around the township.'

They walked into Targo. It had been quiet the previous day, but now it was a complete ghost town.

Cars were parked on the main street, but none were on the road. One vehicle still had its engine running.

'Hello!' Dan yelled.

His voice echoed up and down the street.

'This is creepy,' Ebony said. 'Where is everyone?'

They headed over to Bobby's Diner. No-one was behind the counter. Half-eaten meals were at three of the tables. The jukebox played *Hound Dog* by Elvis. The sound of sizzling came from the kitchen. Chad climbed over the counter and took a look. The grill was on—two beef patties were still cooking—with the makings of a burger to one side.

'Great,' Dan said. 'Everyone's missing except us.'

Chad glanced over at Dan. The younger boy was pale. Gripping his shoulder, Chad said, 'It'll be okay, buddy. No matter what's going on, we'll get through it.'

Brodie nodded. 'Chad's right,' she said. 'We've been through much worse than this. We've got each other, and we're not hurt.'

'That's right,' Ebony said, giving them a rueful grin. 'Except for where I got shot back at New Haven. But even that's okay.'

She pulled back her sleeve and gingerly touched the bandage. 'There's no pain at all,' she said, easing the bandage back, and frowning. 'That's strange.'

Ebony pulled off the bandage. A few days before, the wound had been a bloody mess. Now it was impossible to tell she'd even been shot. 'There's not even a mark,' she said.

'No mark?' Chad said, frowning. Their accelerated healing processes were a byproduct of being modified, but it still should have taken weeks for the wound to completely heal. 'There's got to be something. A scar, at least.'

'There's nothing.'

'That's weird,' Dan said. 'Too weird.'

Brodie shook her head. 'None of this makes any sense,' she said. 'The house. The ghostly happenings in the town. Getting transported to a different dimension.'

'And now the wall,' Chad pointed out. 'It's as if someone's playing with us.'

They left the diner.

'When were things last normal?' Brodie asked.

'New Haven,' Dan said, shrugging.

'After that, Ferdy started losing power.'

'Was your arm still hurting when we arrived here?' Chad asked Ebony.

'Big time,' she said.

'When was the last time you remember it being painful?'

Ebony stroked her chin. 'It was painful when we left *Liber8tor*,' she said. 'We walked through the forest, saw Mavis out the front of her house. Then we went inside—'

'It was still painful then?'

'I think so,' she said. 'Visiting Mavis that first time is all a bit of a haze. I think I fell asleep.'

Chad's throat went dry. 'You fell asleep?' he said. 'I did too.'

Brodie paled. 'I thought it was just me. After

pouring us that lemonade, she gave us her life story. I nodded off .'

They all looked at Dan.

'Yep,' he said. 'Me too.'

'And later,' Brodie said to Ebony, 'was your arm still hurting?'

'No,' Ebony said, frowning. 'It wasn't. When Chad saw the face at the window, I remember thinking that my arm was feeling fine. In fact,' she added, 'it was more than fine. It didn't hurt at all.'

'So what happened when we all nodded off?' Chad asked. 'What happened to the world?'

Brodie drew a sharp breath. 'No,' she said, staring into the distance. 'No, it can't be.'

'What?'

She looked around at the sky, the street and finally at each of the others. 'But it makes sense. The haunted town. The laws of physics being ripped apart at the seams. And the missing population. From the time we dozed off, the world went mad.'

'So what happened?' Chad asked. 'What happened while we slept?'

'Nothing,' Brodie said. 'The world is the same as it's always been. It's us that's changed.' She stared at them in horror. 'We're still asleep.'

Chapter Twenty-Eight

'What?' Chad said. 'We're still...asleep?'

Brodie nodded. It all made sense. It explained why everything had turned topsy-turvy. 'There was something in that lemonade,' she said. 'A drug that knocked us out.'

'So,' Dan said, looking around. 'I'm asleep? And you're all just part of my imagination?'

'Not quite,' Brodie said. 'At least, I don't think so.' She let out a long breath. 'I think we're all sharing the same dream.'

'That's crazy,' Chad said.

'It's not. And it explains everything that's happened since we dozed off at Mavis's house.' She tapped her chin. 'I read an article recently about plans to send astronauts on long voyages to other star systems. People who are asleep use less resources: water, air and food. Upon reaching their destination, they'd be brought out of deep sleep and ready to resume their mission.'

'That doesn't explain how we're sharing the same dream,' Ebony pointed out.

Brodie nodded. 'Scientists have talked about creating a simulated environment where astronauts can exist while they're asleep,' she said. 'Their brains are hooked up to a machine and a program is run where they engage with each other as if it's the real world.'

Chad frowned. 'This is hardly like the real world,' he said.

'You can have any program you want,' Brodie said. 'This could be one of a million.'

'It makes sense,' Dan said, thoughtfully. 'Look at all the strange things that have happened. The haunted house. The weird town. And this wall that seemed to come from nowhere. This can't be reality.'

Pinching herself, Ebony said, 'It *feels* like reality.'

'How can we know for sure?' Chad asked.

Brodie thought for a moment. 'I've got an idea,' she said. 'Dan, you went to the library yesterday?'

'I'll show you where it is.'

They walked the length of the street to the building. Climbing the front steps, they tried the doors.

'Locked,' Chad said.

'Isn't that convenient,' Brodie responded. 'Almost as if they don't want us going in.'

She smashed the glass and they stepped into the cool interior.

'We're going to play a game,' Brodie said. 'Everyone grab a book.'

They all selected books from the shelves.

'Open your books,' Brodie said.

They did. Three jaws dropped open at the same time.

'This is blank,' Dan said.

'Mine too,' Chad said.

'And mine,' Ebony added.

'They're blank because the program didn't know what books you were going to select,' Brodie explained. 'Now we're going to pick something else. Hmm, maybe one of the classics.'

She strode over to a shelf and removed *A Tale*

of Two Cities.

'What do you know about that?' she mused, reading. '*It was the best of times, it was the worst of times.*' She snapped it shut. 'When the system knows what to expect, it knows what to load. It doesn't know how to load unknowns, such as the books you picked at random.'

'This is crazy,' Chad muttered. 'But it fits together.'

'The question is, how do we get out of here?' Ebony said. 'How do we wake up?'

'I've been thinking about that,' Brodie said. 'Clearly the program controls everything external to ourselves; the temperature, the taste of food, anything that isn't us.

'But it doesn't control us. The choices we make. Our free will. I think there might be a way to shock us—or at least me—free from the program.'

'How's that?'

'Hit me.'

'Huh?'

'As hard as you can,' Brodie said. 'Hit me as

if you really mean it.'

'Brodie, I can't—'

'It's for our own benefit!' she snapped. 'Now, hit me!'

Chad drew back a fist and punched her in the face. Brodie fell backwards to the ground, but she saw something as she fell. A ceiling. A computer on a table. Rubbing her jaw, she weaved to her feet. 'Again! And this time like you mean it!'

This time Chad hit her so hard she was airborne. Hitting the ground, she saw the ceiling again, a plain white plasterboard ceiling, and a computer on a desk. She bit hard on the inside of her cheek, so hard she tasted blood. With all her might, she struggled to push aside the world of Targo.

Focusing on the pain, she felt something in the back of her neck. Pulling hard at it, she felt an agony so excruciating she almost blacked out. But she fought against it, rejoiced in the pain, allowed it to flow through her body until—

—a doctor struggled to push her back onto the table. Drawing back a fist, she slammed him in the face. His head jerked back and he fell out of sight. Groaning, Brodie rolled, and crashed off a gurney onto a floor. Pain radiated through her face as her nose contacted with the ground.

She staggered to her feet as another lab technician came crashing through the door.

'No,' she grunted. 'You're not going to stop me.'

Smashing him into a wall, Brodie turned her attention to the other gurneys in the room. Chad, Ebony and Dan had a bunch of wires leading into plugs at the backs of their necks.

Sorry, she thought. *But there's no time to be gentle here.*

Snatching out the plugs, each of them convulsed in pain. As they slowly began to stir, Brodie gingerly touched the top of her spine. There was only a dab of blood, but she'd have a hell of a headache in the morning.

Chad climbed from the table. 'Brodie,' he groaned. 'Are we...are we...'

'Out? Yes, I think so.'

They helped Dan and Ebony off the tables. Ebony looked as if she were about to throw up. 'I feel awful,' she groaned. 'Leave me here to die.'

'That's not allowed,' Chad said.

Brodie glanced at Ebony's wound where she had been shot. It was healing as normal.

They raced from the room, entering a basement where computers lined the walls. Two security guards crashed through the doorway. Raising guns, they fired, but Chad had an ice barricade up in time to deflect the bullets. Ebony created two iron disks from the air and Dan flung them at the men, knocking them out.

Racing up the stairs, Brodie took out another guard at the top. She pushed open another door and they found themselves on the first floor of the Cooper house. A moment later they were outside.

'Look!' Dan yelled.

Hurrying down the road towards them was Mavis. Smiling reassuringly at them, she gave a small wave as her sides exploded into two pairs of insect-like robotic legs. The ends of her arms and legs grew into four robot legs. Her torso expanded into a huge metallic abdomen as her head split open in the middle, revealing a shining jawed mouth and two antenna. Now ten times larger, her human skin hung off her like ripped clothing.

'Well,' Chad said, swallowing hard, 'that's something you don't see every day.'

Chapter Twenty-Nine

Mavis—or the thing that had been the old lady—aimed her antenna at them.

'Duck!' Brodie yelled.

They jumped aside as darts flew past them, one missing Brodie by inches. She snatched up a rock and threw it at the creature. It hit Mavis in her left eye, but didn't slow her down. She leapt towards them, knocking them aside. Chad shot a blast of fire at Mavis, but missed. Ebony formed a metal plate from the air. Dan propelled it at the creature, destroying the two antenna.

Mavis charged forward, knocking Brodie over. Rolling under the robot body, Brodie kicked upwards into her torso, but with no effect. She scrambled away from the rampaging legs, picked up another rock and hurled it, hitting Mavis's right eye. This time the woman hesitated, blinking as she tried to decide who to attack next.

By now, Chad had picked himself up. He fired a blast of ice at one limb, freezing it, as Ebony grabbed another, turning it to carbon. Mavis swung a limb about, smashing Ebony down. Dan slammed the metal disk into Mavis's neck—and her head flew off.

But it didn't stop her.

She charged at Dan, trampling over him as Chad fired a super hot blast at her torso. Boiling hot metal flew off her as he increased the heat, cutting straight through. Mavis ineffectually waved her remaining limbs about before taking a last shuddering step—and expiring.

Brodie picked herself up, groaning. She hobbled over to Ebony, helped her up and they raced over to Dan. He lay on his back, staring up at the sky.

'Dan!' Ebony cried. 'Are you okay?'

'As good as can be expected,' he moaned, 'considering I've been run over by a robotic spider.'

Chad joined them. 'What on earth was that thing?' he asked.

'I've got no idea,' Brodie said. 'But I hope there's only one of them.' There was something niggling in the back of her mind, something that gave her an odd sense of unease. 'Let's just get back to *Liber8tor*. The sooner we're out of here, the better.'

They ran through the woods. Minutes later they reached the ship. Brodie let out of a sigh of relief. It seemed like years since they had last seen *Liber8tor*. They climbed aboard and took their positions on the bridge.

'Ferdy!' Dan yelled. 'Initiate engines! We've got to get out of here.'

But there was no response. Glancing at a control panel, Dan said, '*Liber8tor*'s power levels are critically low!'

'Can we get out of here?' Chad asked.

'Yes, but it looks like Ferdy's offline.'

'Let's go,' Brodie said. 'We'll reactivate Ferdy later.'

Dan started the engines. As they warmed up, the ground started to shake violently under the ship.

Ebony frowned at her controls. 'I'm getting something on the radar,' she said. 'Something's moving under us. Get us out of here!'

'The engines are sluggish,' Dan said. 'Not sure how fast we can go.'

They lifted off. The view screen showed the

landscape, violently shaking, as if struck by a huge earthquake. Then it seemed to fall away completely, revealing a huge hole in the ground with a slithering shape moving about at the bottom.

'Go!' Chad shouted.

The engines surged, but then a huge, tentacle reached from the pit. It slammed into *Liber8tor*, the vessel slewed sideways and Brodie heard the smashing of branches as they scraped the tops of the trees.

'I'm giving the engines everything,' Dan said, 'but we're still not—'

Crash!

Brodie was thrown from her seat and across the bridge. *Whack!* Her head hit a console and she saw stars. The next thing she knew, Chad was dragging her across the floor.

'What...what's happening?' she slurred.

'That thing slapped us down,' he said. 'We crashed.'

Groaning, Brodie struggled to her feet. The bridge was in near darkness except for the view screen that showed a close-up of the creature. It appeared huge.

'Are the weapons still online?' she asked.

'Only just,' Chad said.

'Then target the middle of that...thing and shoot!'

Chad settled behind his console. Swiping a few controls, he said, 'Readying missiles,' he said. 'And...firing!' *Liber8tor* shook as the missile left the ship. There was an explosion. 'That's a direct hit!'

'Is it dead?'

Extricating herself from beneath a shattered console, Ebony examined her screen. 'I think so,' she said. 'Unless it can get through life without a head.'

Dan appeared from behind another console and joined them as they climbed from *Liber8tor*. The ship had crashed inside the pit. A support leg was broken, and part of the hull badly dented. On the other side of the pit was the monster, a beast with razor-sharp teeth and tentacles.

Brodie shuddered as she peered at it. There were no eyes visible. It must have had some sort of internal radar system.

'Where do the bad guys get these things?' Dan asked. 'There must be a monster version of Ebay where they shop.'

'We do seem to run into a lot of weird creatures,' Ebony agreed. 'It's a good thing you made a direct hit on its head—or what passes for a head. Taking out a tentacle would have still left it with another seven.'

'An eight-armed monster,' Chad said, shaking his head with disbelief. 'Great.'

A chill went through Brodie. 'What did you say?' she asked.

'What?' He stared at her. 'I was just saying it's got eight arms...or legs...or whatever they are.'

'Eight,' Brodie said the word, her mouth dry. 'Of course there's eight. What else would there be?'

The others were staring at her. 'Are you all right?' Ebony asked. 'You hit your head pretty hard.'

'I'm fine,' she said. 'But we're not.'

'What do you mean?'

'Have you noticed how many times we've

encountered the number eight?' she asked.

'Uh, not really,' Dan said.

'The dining room back at the Cooper house had eight chairs,' Brodie said.

'Nothing weird about that.'

'And the guy back at the diner—Eric—had owned the place for eight years.' Brodie thought hard. 'Dan, didn't you say those dogs that chased you had—'

'—eight legs.'

'And the ship I was on,' Ebony said, thoughtfully. 'It was named *The Eight Hands*.'

'Chad?' Brodie said. 'And you?'

'There wasn't anything...' His voice trailed off. 'It can't mean anything,' he said, as if trying to convince himself. 'But a lady at the supermarket was buying a jumbo pack of cereal for eight dollars...and the supermarket had eight aisles.'

'And it was an eight-sided wall surrounding Exetor,' Brodie said. 'And what did Mavis turn into?'

'An eight-legged robot,' Dan said, puzzled. 'But what does it mean?'

'It means the program has an error,' Brodie said. 'A very simple, almost unnoticeable error, but still an error.'

'What are you talking about?' Chad said. 'We're out of the program.'

'No, we're not,' Brodie said. 'We didn't wake up in a lab under the house. We didn't fight Mavis or get smacked down by an eight-armed monster. We're still inside the software.'

Chapter Thirty

'How very clever of you.'

Brodie and the others looked around. The voice had seemed to come from everywhere at once. Then the pit, *Liber8tor* and the dead creature shimmered, paled and they were standing in Targo's main street. The walls still surrounded the town, but there was no sign of the populace. Exetor looked like it had been abandoned for years, leaving it a ghost town.

The ground shook. They looked at each other in alarm as it shuddered again and again as loud thuds grew closer.

'Look!' Ebony said, pointing behind them.

A man—a hundred feet tall—was walking across the landscape towards them, making the ground shake with every step. He destroyed everything in his path, crushing houses, trees and cars.

He wore a pale gray suit, shiny business shoes and round-rimmed lenses. But it was his face that was most frightening. Burnt in a fire, his hair was completely missing and his eyes wide. His nose had been reduced to a melted nub of flesh and his ears were completely gone.

'And here are the children,' he said, staring down at them. 'The ones who thought they would destroy my life.'

The man had a faint German accent. Brodie thought it sounded oddly familiar. She knew that voice—but from where?

The giant slowly shrunk. Within seconds he stood before them, a little taller than themselves. He nodded to Brodie. 'You have done well, little one,' he said. 'There was a glitch in programming. We had hoped you would not notice.'

'Who are you?' Brodie asked.

'It makes no difference who I am.'

'She asked you a question,' Chad snapped. 'What's your name?'

'Ah,' the man mused. 'The boy speaks. He does not remember me, but I remember him.'

Chad stared at him in confusion.

'Oh no,' Brodie said. 'Ravana.'

Not long after she and the others had been modified, they had been captured by an organization called Typhoid. Doctor Ravana, an insidious doctor, had tortured them for information. While escaping, Chad had fired a blast of fire at him, enveloping him in flames. Later, Ebony had turned him to salt.

Inexplicably, he had survived.

The same thoughts must have gone through Chad's mind too. Without warning, Chad pointed it at Ravana and fired a blast of ice at him. The doctor merely laughed as the ice stopped inches away from him and angled towards the ground.

'We're not in your world now, boy,' Ravana said. 'You're in mine.'

Chad's powers failed completely. The others tried their powers, but they didn't work. They couldn't move either. Their feet were stuck to the ground.

'You'll move when I allow you to move,' Ravana said, 'and not an instant before.'

'Why are we here?' Brodie asked. 'What's going on?'

'Surely that is obvious. This is about revenge. A kind of revenge from which there is no escape. When your friend, Chad, destroyed my appearance with fire, I decided I would pay you back for what you had done.'

'But I killed you,' Ebony said. 'How can you be alive?'

'I cannot die,' Ravana said, mysteriously. 'That explanation will suffice—for now.'

'What are we doing here?' Dan asked.

'After the collapse of Typhoid, I was left with little in the way of money or resources,' Ravana said. 'It was necessary for me to acquire partners with whom I could work to bring about your downfall.

'Your friend, Axel, believes he is living with his newfound family. They are, of course, completely bogus. Their mission is to gain his trust and encourage him to join an organization be believes is called Rescue Prime. They are actually a band of mercenaries. I know not of their plans for him. My ambitions would have been complete if I could have destroyed him too, but, alas, it was not to be.'

He's completely insane, Brodie thought.

'I was able to broker a rather more favorable deal with an organization known as Force-One. My proposal to them was simple. The adrenalin created by your brains can be synthesized into a potion that can give people superpowers.

'Certainly, those powers would not be as powerful as your own, or as long lived, but in that lies the advantage. Many people will pay vast sums of money to buy your powers. Their short term effects will enable people to rob banks, murder those who have stood against them and carry out their heart's desire.

'At one million dollars per shot, it is a small price to pay for such power.'

Brodie's mind was reeling. Ravena's words made sense. There *were* plenty of people who would pay big dollars to have superpowers—even if they were temporary.

'So...what is this place?' she asked. 'And where are our bodies?'

'You're consciousness is inside a program

called Terminal Fear,' Ravana explained, 'while your bodies are held in a lab, sedated, connected to machines that monitor your vitals. Nutrients are fed into your blood streams. Waste matter is removed. When you sleep here, you sleep in the real world. When you wake here, your brains awaken to a new day.'

'How long will we be prisoners here?' Ebony asked, aghast.

Doctor Ravana chuckled. 'For as long as you live,' he said. 'Theoretically, you could be kept alive for decades, possibly even centuries—'

'You monster!' Brodie yelled.

She struggled to move, but was held fast.

'Please don't bother,' Ravana said, smiling. 'You'll only hurt yourself. Oh,' he added, 'you *can* hurt yourself. As you've already discovered, you can be harmed here. Killed, even, although if you should die here, you will be brought back.' The smile broadened. 'We have invested a lot in you. We want to milk your adrenal glands for many years to come.'

Brodie wanted to tear the man limb from limb.

'Doctor,' Chad said. He had gone pale. 'If it's me you blame for your condition, then...I'm sorry. Let the others go—'

'That's very noble of you,' Ravana said. 'But your friends will pay for your misdeeds for some time to come. Stress, excitement and fear stimulate the adrenal gland. You can expect to receive plenty of that in the years—and decades—ahead.'

Ravana turned and, walking away, disappeared into thin air. At the same time, Brodie and the others found they could move.

'What a horrible man,' Ebony said.

'He won't be on my Christmas card list,' Dan muttered.

'How will we get out of here?' Brodie asked.

'I don't know,' Chad said, his chin quivering. 'We may be stuck here for the rest of our lives—and it's all my fault.'

Chapter Thirty-One

'So how do we get in?' I asked.

We were in an abandoned house opposite Wilson Electrics. Three vans were parked outside the factory. Quinn had said there were never less than a dozen men there at any time. I could launch a full scale attack on the complex, but I didn't want them to know I was privy to their scheme. Quinn and I had already gone into town where I'd left my watch at the movies to make it look like we were catching a show.

'The place is heavily guarded,' Quinn said. 'I thought about disguising myself as one of the staff, but I didn't know where they were keeping my dad.'

A truck drove down the street towards the front gates. 'There,' I said. 'We'll hitch a ride.'

Racing after the truck, I used my powers to levitate us onto the roof. Landing gently, we heard the truck slow as it reached the main building. It stopped. Two men left the building as a group of teenagers climbed from the rear.

Quinn and I exchanged glances.

What's this all about?

I nudged her. This was our chance. We floated down the opposite side of the truck and joined the group. No-one seemed to notice our presence. It was obvious these people barely knew each other.

'Welcome to Processing,' one man said. He had a mustache and a crew cut. 'I'm Commander Shaw. I'll be taking you through the first stage.' He indicated his companion, a stocky clean-shaved man. 'This is Sergeant Tanner. He'll take you to Induction.'

Tanner stepped forward. 'If anyone's having any second thoughts,' he said, 'now's the time to drop out. No-one will think any the less of you.'

The crowd was completely motionless. Then a skinny guy, a little older than me, cautiously raised his hand.

'Your name?' Tanner said.

'John Henley,' he said. 'I don't think this is for me. I—'

Tanner produced a gun. Without hesitation, he trained it on Henley and shot him. The crowd cried out as the youth flew backwards onto the dusty ground—dead. Pocketing the weapon, Tanner turned to everyone.

'That's what happens to quitters,' he said. 'You're either completely with us, or you're completely against us. There's no middle ground. Does anyone have any questions.' No-one did. 'Then follow me.'

We trailed him into the factory. It had once been used to manufacture radios and televisions, but hadn't been used for decades. Passing benches with pieces of old wire and tools on them, I wondered why they had decided to use this factory as their base of operations.

It didn't take long to find out. Leading us down a flight of stairs, Tanner flashed a badge at an ID scanner and the door slid open. We walked onto a mezzanine level overlooking a huge chamber. People were working on flying ships, similar in design to the Flex craft owned by The Agency. Others were test firing weapons at targets.

What was this place?

Tanner led us to a meeting room. Stepping onto a small stage to speak, we settled behind desks. Staying near Quinn, I saw her hands shaking. I gave her a small nod.

Everything will be fine.

I hoped.

Glancing over the top of Tanner, I saw a logo on the wall, an 'E' surrounded by a circle. *Holy Hell*, I thought. *This is—*

'Welcome to E-Group,' Tanner said. 'Today begins your training that will help enable us to retake the earth from the EDs—economic dictators—that have stolen it from the common people.'

It seemed like a lifetime had passed since we had encountered the terrorist group on the Sydney Harbor Bridge. Considering they were against the modern world, they didn't seem to mind making use of every modern technology they could get their hands on.

'You have arrived at an exciting time. Our attacks against the EDs have grown in intensity over the last few months. All it will require is a single good push, and the capitalist countries of the world will once again fall back into the hands of the people.'

This guy's an idiot, I thought.

The world was a big place. Attacking famous landmarks wouldn't topple governments. If anything, it had united people, making them more resolute against E-Group. The other members of the group, however, seemed intoxicated by his words. They broke into rapturous applause. Exchanging glances, Quinn and I followed suit.

'Power across the globe has been held by those with money. Working with governments and organizations like the newly revealed Agency, their aim is to stifle the common people, to crush us beneath their boot.

'But that is about to change.' Tanner paused dramatically. 'Soon unbridled power will be in your hands. Soon the world will falter as we unleash Hell upon it.' He turned to Shaw. 'Turn on the monitor.'

Shaw crossed to a console and pressed a switch. A television screen flickered on, showing static, then an image of a man sitting in a cell.

Quinn drew a sharp breath. Glancing over, I saw her face turn pale. It must have been her father, Robert Okada.

'This man's daughter is currently on assignment for us, although she is not a believer. She is able to shape shift. Once she returns, we will be synthesizing a formula from her genes.' He turned to the audience. 'Can you imagine what we can achieve as a group with the power to shape shift? Can you conceive of the number of world leaders we could assassinate in one place at one time with those powers?

'And that's just the beginning. Plans are currently underway to develop serums from a number of other modified humans.'

A girl near the front put up her hand. 'When will the serums be ready?' she asked.

'Within days.'

Another boy raised an arm. 'What is our target?

Tanner smiled. It was an ugly grin. 'That

information is classified,' he said, 'for now. But I promise we will strike where the planet's economic leaders meet, and the world will watch their final downfall.'

Shaw went over to Tanner and murmured something. Tanner turned back to the audience.

'It is time you were taken to your quarters,' he said. 'We will familiarize you with the process before delivering the injections.'

The monitor snapped off. We filed out the door and Shaw led us down a corridor towards the heart of the complex. Remaining at the rear of the group, I grabbed Quinn and dragged her into a broom cupboard.

'That was your father on the monitor?' I asked.

'Yes!' Quinn hissed. 'We need to find him.'

'That's easier said than done. This is a big place. He could be anywhere.'

'I've got an idea,' she said. 'We'll need access to a computer.'

Leaving the cupboard, we made our way back

to the meeting room. Hurrying over to a computer on the far side, Quinn sat at the desk and started punching keys.

'What are you looking for?' I asked.

'You know what a zeno emitter does?'

Did I ever? The devices could nullify our powers. They had been used more than once to render us helpless.

'Zeno emitters use an enormous amount of energy,' Quinn explained. 'It takes a lot of infrastructure to operate them.' She pointed to a schematic on the screen. 'You see these reinforced conduits leading to the basements? They're probably designed to hold modified humans down there. It must be where they're holding my father.'

'We've just got to—'

I stopped. Footsteps approached and the door was pushed open. Shaw appeared in the doorway.

'What the hell are you doing here?' he growled.

Chapter Thirty-Two

For what seemed like an eternity—but was probably only about five seconds—my mouth opened and closed like a fish. Then I heard a voice from beside me.

'This recruit's with me.'

Glancing down, I saw Tanner on the seat beside me.

What the—?

How could Tanner have come into the room? And why was he now defending me? Then I realized. It was Quinn! She had transformed herself into the E-Group leader!

'This recruit had some extra questions,' Quinn continued. 'I decided to run through them with him.'

'The briefing downstairs is just about to start,' Shaw said. 'Don't you think—'

'Leave the thinking to me. I'll bring him shortly.'

'Of course, sir.'

Shaw left. 'And to think I kissed you,' I said to Tanner. 'I must have been out of my head.'

'I didn't have a mustache then,' she said. 'Come on. Let's go.'

Quinn stayed disguised as Tanner as we made our way along a corridor and down a flight of stairs. Reaching the basement, she lowered her eye to an iris scanner. The door clicked open.

'That's pretty impressive,' I said.

'I'm an impressive girl.'

We entered a lab. Scientists were standing at benches, mixing potions and entering information on computers. Security guards lining the walls nodded at Quinn, thinking she was Tanner. Reaching a locked door at the end, she tried her eye on another security scanner, but it buzzed impotently. She tried again. It would not open.

'Tanner?'

The voice came from a man in a lab coat, whose badge identified him as Harper. He had been examining a Petri dish under a microscope. On the wall to his right was a large red button with an *Emergency* sign under it.

'Ah, good,' Quinn said, trying to sound

official. 'I need to see the prisoner.'

'Which one?'

'Okada.'

Harper looked at him curiously. 'You know your security level doesn't allow you into the labs,' he said. Turning to me, he added, 'And who is this?'

'A new recruit. He's a modified human. I believe he'll be able to get information out of Okada.'

'How could you forget about the security arrangements?' Harper asked, frowning.

'I've had a lot on my mind,' Quinn said, her voice going high. 'Now stop wasting my time and let us through.'

'I understand that,' Harper soothed. 'I was just surprised because it was you who insisted we upgrade security.'

'I know.'

Harper slapped the alarm system, and the siren rang throughout the complex. 'It was *me* who insisted on upgrading security,' he snapped. 'Who are you? What are—'

I arrowed a fist into his chin and he slumped

to the floor. The alarm ringing loudly in our ears, I focused on expanding the air in the gap between the door and the frame. Metal sheered as it broke free. Running footsteps came from behind, and two guards opened fire.

Blocking the hail of bullets with an air wall, I dragged Quinn through the doorway and jammed the door into the frame. It would hold, but not for long.

We raced down a corridor. There were doors on each side. Peering through the small window of one near the end, Quinn let out a shriek. 'It's Dad!' she yelled. 'He's in here.'

I jerked the door off its hinges and we entered. Robert Okada was a Japanese man with a broad, honest face. His black hair was streaked with gray, but he looked about forty.

He leapt up. 'What?' he said. 'Who are you? Where—'

Quinn shape shifted into her normal self, a slim Japanese girl with bright eyes and pretty lips. 'Dad!' she said. 'We're here to save you!'

He hugged Quinn tightly before his eyes

angled to me. 'And this is—?'

'Axel,' I said, 'but we don't have time for a reunion right now. We've got to escape.'

Footsteps were charging down the corridor.

I fired cannonballs made of compressed air at half-a-dozen guards. It knocked them flying and they didn't move. Still, I felt no confidence about getting up to the next level. If it had just been me, I may have been able to do it, but getting Quinn and her father out as well would be almost impossible.

'There may be another way,' Mr Okada said. 'I notice the smell down here was quite bad.'

'I don't understand—'

'There are old sewers that flow directly under this basement. We can use them to escape.'

I spotted a grill set into the floor. Mr Okada was right about the smell. It was bad, all right, but the sewers might just spell the difference between life and death. Expanding the gaps between the bars, I cracked open the floor and lowered us into the sewer. There was just one problem. No light.

Quinn solved this by producing a cell phone

and using the torch app. Within seconds we were racing down the passageway to an intersection.

Mr Okada pointed to the left. 'This way,' he said. 'It should lead to the street.'

We hurried to the end where a metal ladder led up. At the top, I shoved aside a manhole cover and emerged. The wire fence was behind us. Armed men were running from the building. I threw up a barrier as they fired on us.

'Come on!' I yelled to Quinn and her father. Creating a raft of air, we climbed onto it and swept into the sky.

A ship, similar to a flex craft, took off from a warehouse and fired. Avoiding the missile, I launched an air cannonball at its engine, spinning the vessel about. It lurched towards ground, smoke trailing from it.

'Axel!' Quinn yelled, pointing to an antenna on one of the buildings. 'Destroy that!'

There was no time to argue. More armed men were already streaming from the building. I used a burst of air to reduce the antenna to scrap. With bullets flying all around us, I flew us away from the factory.

'What was all that about?' I asked Quinn.

'What?'

'The antenna.'

'Oh,' she said. 'Check your comm bracelet.'

I did. For the first time in days, I had a clear signal. *Liber8tor* was sending an automated distress signal.

'I've got to put you down,' I said to Quinn and Mr Okada. 'My friends need me.'

'We'll come with you,' Mr Okada said. 'It's the least we can do after risking your life for us.'

'It might be dangerous.'

'I've faced a lot of danger over the years,' Mr Okada said, mysteriously. 'A little more won't hurt.'

Putting on a burst of speed, I took us in the direction of the signal.

'I just hope I'm not too late,' I said.

Chapter Thirty-Three

Two hours later, we were flying over dense woods in northern Virginia. I kept checking the comm bracelet, trying to communicate with the others, but there was no response. Quinn placed a hand on my arm.

'We'll be there soon,' she said.

'I know,' I said. 'But I'm worried.' Especially after what Tanner had said about developing serums from other mods. 'This distress signal would only be transmitted in an emergency.'

'How far are we from your vessel?' Mr Okada asked.

'Less than a mile, now.'

'May I make a suggestion? Discretion may be the better part of valor. It may be safer to put down here and walk.'

It was a good idea. Landing, we crept through the forest, following the signal of the bracelet. Within half-an-hour, we found *Liber8tor*. The vessel was de-cloaked and surrounded by armed guards. A few scientists were working on an entry door, trying to open it.

Ferdy had recorded a power loss when I had last seen the team. Had *Liber8tor* completely run out of energy? But how was the ship still sending a message? And where were Brodie and the others?

'How will we get in?' Quinn asked.

'I don't know.'

Mr Okada rubbed his chin thoughtfully. 'I wonder what would happen if you tried contacting your ship again,' he said. 'Someone may be aboard.'

I did this. 'This is Axel,' I said. 'I'm outside the ship. If anyone's in there—'

That was as far as I got. A burst of electricity flew from the ship like a crackling whip, hitting the scientists and the guards. They collapsed into a heap on the ground.

Liber8tor's lower door opened and we boarded.

'Ferdy?' I ventured.

'Axel,' Ferdy's voice came back. 'It is indeed good to hear your voice.'

'What's happening?'

'*Liber8tor's* power levels are at two percent. The power drain must be stopped immediately or the ship will be permanently inoperable.'

'What do I need to do?'

'Ferdy has ascertained that the power loss is due to a device on the underneath of the hull.'

We scrambled under the ship and began searching. After a few minutes, I wondered if Ferdy were wrong.

'There's nothing here,' I said. 'It looks the same as usual.'

'A device might be attached that's invisible to the naked eye,' Mr Okada said. 'Is there any way you can test for that?'

One advantage of being able to control air is that I can also create a vacuum. Using a strong suction, I removed all the air along the bottom of the hull. Nothing happened, but then I focused on sucking every last atom from the surface of the metal.

Klang!

A metal disk hit the ground.

'What is that?' Quinn asked.

'Nothing good,' I replied, crushing it.

Hitting my comm bracelet, I asked Ferdy how long it would take to recover.

'Several hours,' he said. 'And the capitol of Norway is Oslo.'

'Does he always do that?' Quinn asked.

'Ferdy's a barrel of information.'

I asked him about the others.

'They have been gone for several days,' he said. 'Ferdy sent out repeated messages, both to you and the other crew members, but without success.'

'I've been off the air,' I said. 'Long story. What was the last location of the crew?'

'They headed towards the town of Targo,' he said.

Finding a trail, Quinn and her father followed me. I didn't want to fly over the town for risk of drawing attention to myself. We reached a road with a cemetery on one side and a couple of houses on the other. The first place looked ready to fall over. The other had a more lived in feel. A white van was parked in front.

I had a sense of disquiet as I looked at the van, but I didn't know why.

'That's a new van,' Quinn said.

She had hit the nail on the head.

It was a late model vehicle. Not that people couldn't drive new cars around, but this seemed like an odd van to have sitting around on a quiet street in the middle of nowhere.

'Let me do this,' I said to the others. 'Things might get a little unpleasant.'

'I'll come with you,' Quinn said. 'A shape shifter might come in handy.'

'You're not leaving me behind,' Mr Okada said.

I sighed. 'Okay,' I said. 'Just don't get shot...or stabbed...or anything.'

Marching up to the front door, I knocked and waited. It was only seconds before an old lady appeared. She looked alarmed.

'Yes?'

'Sorry to bother you,' I said. 'Some friends of mine have gone missing and I'm trying to track them down.'

'Really?' Her voice went up an octave. 'Perhaps you should come in. Have a glass of lemonade.'

The old lady led us into a parlor. Giving us a nervous smile, she disappeared through a door. Glancing about, I looked around for anything that appeared amiss, but it all looked startlingly normal. I was beginning to think we were on completely the wrong track when—

'Look out!' Mr Okada yelled.

As he pushed me aside, I saw the old lady in the doorway. A gun went off in her hand, and I retaliated with a blast of air that knocked her out.

'So much for little old ladies,' I said, picking myself up off the floor. 'Her lemonade must have been—'

Oh no.

Quinn's father was on the floor, a bullet wound in the middle of his forehead. He had saved my life, but at the cost of his own. I grabbed his wrist, desperate to find a pulse. I felt none.

'Quinn!' I said. 'I'm so sorry. I didn't mean for this to happen—'

'Axel,' she said, kneeling next to me. 'It's okay. Really.'

I couldn't understand how she could be so calm.

'It's not!' I cried. 'I don't know how you can be so calm—'

'All is fine.'

The voice didn't come from Quinn. Turning in astonishment, I saw Mr Okada blinking. Sitting up, the wound in his head slowly closed up, the bullet pushed out and plopped onto the floorboards.

'How...what...' I stammered.

'It's a long story,' he said. 'And there's no time to explain right now. That shot may have alerted others.'

Almost in response, I heard the sound of footsteps approaching the rear of the house. Armed guards crashed through the doorway. This time I was prepared, taking them out with a barrage of air balls. We raced through the building. Computers, and boxes of chemicals, filled the kitchen.

'What is this stuff?' I asked.

'It's hard to say without closer examination,' Mr Okada said. 'But I wonder if that old property up the road has anything to do with this.'

'What makes you say that?'

'There were tire marks in front. I didn't think anything of it at the time, but...'

Within minutes we were striding through the front gate. It was hard to believe anything was going on here—the building looked ready to knock down— but a trail of footsteps in the dust led to the front door. A quick search led us to a brightly lit basement filled with lab equipment, computers—and my friends.

'It's them!' I cried.

Brodie, Chad, Dan and Ebony were attached to a network of computers via a plethora of wires and tubes. They were stationary, except for their eyelids.

'They're in a state of REM,' Mr Okada said, examining them. 'It's a deep-sleep state that people usually experience four or five times a night. I think they're locked into it completely.'

'We need to disconnect them!' I said.

Mr Okada grabbed my arm. 'Let me,' he said. 'I've had medical training.'

'All right. Just be careful—'

'Axel!' Quinn yelled.

She was pointing at a cone-shaped device on a bench. I had just enough time to realize it was a bomb when—

Ka-boom!

Chapter Thirty-Four

It's not easy to contain the blast of an explosion.

Wrapping an air bubble around the bomb just as it exploded took all my strength. The compressed energy was like a miniature tornado, swirling and moving, fighting to escape. If I released it, the blast would expand rapidly, tearing the room apart and killing everyone in it.

'Got to get it out of here,' I grunted.

I maneuvered the bubble of compressed explosion up the stairs ahead of me. One slip in concentration and—goodbye world. Quinn opened doors for me until I made it outside.

Sending the bubble high above the house, I finally released the force of the explosion.

Ka-boom!

Its shockwave threw us to the ground. We slowly stood and looked at each other.

'You're a handy guy to have around,' Quinn said.

'Just doing my job.'

Whoever was behind this had decided to cut their losses and run, leaving no evidence by blowing us to pieces. If I'd been an instant slower...

Well, I didn't want to think about that.

We went back inside. By now, Mr Okada had deactivated the machines and withdrawn the IV leads and oxygen. Leaning over Brodie, I watched her face as the color returned. She blinked slowly, looking into my eyes.

'Is this real?' she asked.

'Or is it all just a dream within a dream?' I asked her. 'It's real, all right.'

Groaning, she sat up. The others were stirring now too.

'Is that you?' Chad asked me. 'I mean, really you?'

'No,' I said. 'I'm just a figment of your imagination.'

'After what we've been through,' he said, 'that's not funny.'

He and the others quickly told me about their time within the Terminal Fear program before I brought them up to date on what I'd been through. Brodie frowned at Quinn and her father.

'Are you sure we can trust you?' she asked.

'We mean you no harm,' Mr Okada said. 'In fact, we want to help.'

'I'm not sure you can,' Ebony said. 'We don't even know what Dr Ravana intended.'

'It sounds like he was intending to sell your synthesized adrenalin to E-Group. I suggest we return there first.'

'Thanks for the suggestion, bud,' Chad said, 'but we don't need your help.'

I could understand his reluctance. Quinn and her father had been partly responsible for everything we'd endured.

'But I hope you'll accept our assistance, anyway,' Mr Okada said, staring at us. 'I believe E-Group are aiming to hit a big target, resulting in the deaths of many innocents. Do you want their blood on your hands?'

Dan spoke up. 'It can't hurt to have these two along,' he said. 'We'll need all the help we can get.'

Grudgingly, Chad nodded. We returned to *Liber8tor* to find the ship fully repowered.

'Ferdy?' I ventured.

'Hello Axel and friends. It is good to have the team back together.'

I explained everything that had happened. 'E-Group talked about hitting a central economic target,' I said. 'Do you have any idea what that could be.'

'Ferdy has a list of possible targets,' he said. 'There are some 9,344,231 possible—'

'Uh,' Dan cut in. 'Could we trim that down a little?'

'Based on what criteria?'

'E-Group are planning to attack soon. Maybe in the next forty-eight hours.'

'Then the list can be shortened to 1,587,231 possible targets.'

This wasn't getting us anywhere.

'It looks like we may have to take the fight to them.'

I gave him the address for Wilson Electrics.

Within seconds Dan had us in the air, and we

were zooming away from Targo. Chad drew me to one side.

'Hey buddy,' he said. 'How're you doing?'

'Fine. Except for these new friends of yours. Are you sure we can trust them?'

I peered past him. Quinn and Mr Okada were speaking to Brodie and Ebony. They burst into laughter at some joke.

'I think so,' I said. 'Mr Okada saved my life.'

'Still...'

I shrugged. 'We've got to be cautious,' I said. 'But aren't we always?'

Chad nodded. We reached Wilson Electrics in under an hour. If we were expecting a fight, we didn't get one. It immediately became obvious that E-Group had packed up and left. Probably our rescue of Mr Okada had pre-empted them. We spent a couple of hours searching the complex, but it had been cleared out. Even the antenna I had wrecked on our departure had been removed.

'They must have had an escape plan worked out in case things went south,' Brodie said. 'Where to now?'

'There's always the family home,' Quinn suggested, raising an eyebrow.

Sighing, I said, 'Let's go.'

But we had no success there either. My "family" had obviously received their marching orders, and were gone too. We searched the house, but found nothing to indicate their plans.

Back on *Liber8tor*, I had an idea. 'Ferdy,' I said. 'You remember those flex ships that were able to follow *Liber8tor*'s heat signature?'

'Ferdy remembers that incident exactly,' Ferdy said. 'The real name of Blackbeard the Pirate was Edward Teach.'

'Thanks. So, what if one of those ships were damaged and trailing some kind of exhaust. Would we be able to follow it?'

'That is possible.'

I directed us back to the factory. The complex looked unchanged.

'I'm deploying senses,' Brodie said. 'Hmm, there's the usual range of pollutants in the air, but there's something more too.'

'What is it?' Chad asked.

'Radiation. Very faint.'

'Ferdy,' Ebony said. 'Is it possible to follow it?'

'It is, indeed.'

'Dan?' I said.

'I'm on it.' Seconds later we were zooming across the landscape. I leant back in my seat as Quinn sat down at an unused astronavigation station. As Ebony explained her console to Mr Okada, I thought back to the farm I thought would be my home.

'The photos back at the house,' I said, turning to Quinn. 'They were...'

'Produced by a graphic design package,' she said. 'They made you look younger. Other people were inserted into the pictures.'

'And Adam Baker and his parents?'

Quinn sighed. 'The safest way to tell a lie is to stick mainly to the truth,' she said. 'Mary and Tom Baker were killed in an accident when they tried to drive through a swollen river. Their son's body was never found.'

'But what if I'd returned to my old town?'

'How could you? You were already a wanted fugitive. The Agency would have come down on you like a ton of bricks.'

'So all of it was a lie,' I said. 'Louise and Henry were pretending to be my aunt and uncle. You were pretending to be my girlfriend.'

'I'm sorry,' Quinn said. 'But I needed to save my father.'

'Speaking of...' I glanced over at Mr Okada. 'There's that little issue of him returning from the dead.'

'Oh. That.'

'Yes. Unless he's a zombie, in which case it'd make complete sense.'

She shook her head. 'He's no zombie.'

'Then—'

'Not yet.'

It seemed I couldn't have all my answers at once.

Chapter Thirty-Five

'We are nearing a property in upstate New York,' Ferdy said.

'It looks like it's a private home,' Dan said. 'Big and surrounded by miles of parkland.'

'If it's E-Group,' I said, 'they must have friends in high places. Real estate around here costs millions.'

'So much for being anti-economy,' Brodie said.

Before I could reply, there was a blast as *Liber8tor* was thrown to one side. The engines whined and lighting flickered as we were tossed to the floor. Only Dan remained in his seat as he struggled to keep us under control.

'We've taken a direct hit!' he yelled. 'One of the port thrusters is wrecked!'

'Ferdy!' I said. 'Weren't we cloaked?'

'*Liber8tor* was cloaked,' Ferdy confirmed. 'They may have been able to target the ship's heat signature.'

We've got to do something about that, I

thought. *Providing we don't get blown up in the next sixty seconds.*

'Another missile is approaching,' Ferdy announced. 'Twenty seconds till impact.'

'Raise the barriers!' I yelled.

'The barriers are off line.'

'Chad! Target that missile!'

Chad dragged himself to the weapon's console. The seconds ticked by. Finally I heard the sound of a missile leaving *Liber8tor*.

Ka-blam!

Our missile collided with the enemy's and exploded.

'I got it!' Chad yelled.

'A second missile has been launched,' Ferdy announced.

'Where're they coming from?' I asked.

'There's a launch pad on the property,' Brodie said. 'Now they've fired a third time.'

'Chad,' I said. 'Target the launch pad. Then take out those two missiles.'

The next few seconds were tense as Chad

fired weapons. Then he yelled, 'The missiles are out of action! And the launch pad is in pieces!'

'We'll be in pieces too if we're not careful,' Dan said. 'The remaining thrusters are overheating.'

'Put us down.'

The ship lurched towards the ground. I couldn't help but be in admiration of Dan's piloting ability. Here he was, a fourteen year old kid, flying like an ace. We came down heavily, but in one piece.

'We're down,' he said, gulping. 'Just.'

'Come on!' I yelled. 'Let's go!'

We were outside in seconds. The building dominating the property was an old fashioned antebellum home with six marble columns lining the front of the portico. Behind them sat a long, flat building with a dozen windows.

A team of black-clad men with guns came streaming through the front door.

It seemed a shame to wreck the house, but it couldn't be helped.

As the men opened fire, I retaliated with a volley of air cannonballs. At the same time, Chad leapt onto his fireboard and shot ball of ice at the house, demolishing the left wing. I threw up a barrier to protect us from gunfire as Ebony made a metal column in midair. Dan propelled it towards the approaching guards.

They were down in seconds. I was surprised we had made such short work of them. Then I realized these guys were just a diversion. A ship lifted off from the rear of the property. Black, and shaped like a ladybird, the vessel fired a scattering of bombs at us.

I formed a barrier, protecting us. The bombs exploded, but only succeeding in killing or injuring their own people. As the black vessel disappeared into the distance, I dropped the barrier and we hurried over to the injured.

'I doubt they care who they kill,' Mr Okada said grimly, as he worked on one of the men. 'They've got bigger fish to fry.'

'They've got to be stopped,' I said. 'But where do they intend to attack?'

'I've been thinking about that. Wasn't there a

major meeting scheduled at the United Nations building today?'

The meeting had been in the news for weeks. 'Most of the world leaders are meeting to discuss the global economy,' I said. 'It's the ideal target for E-Group.'

I leapt into the air. Below me, the beautiful old building had caught fire, my friends were giving first aid to the injured E-Group men and *Liber8tor* looked damaged. Our ship wouldn't be flying any time soon. By then, the whole United Nations building could be in ruins and most of the world leaders dead.

I flew away from the scene. The black vessel had already soared away, out of sight. For several minutes, I flew without seeing it, then realized I didn't need to do this alone.

Hitting my comm bracelet, I said, 'Ferdy? Are you there?'

'Ferdy is here, friend Axel,' his voice came back.

I quickly explained my mission.

'The vessel is moving away from you on a North-Easterly trajectory at Mach Two.'

Mach Two. That was twice the speed of sound. Thanking Ferdy, I disconnected and put on an extra burst of speed. Within minutes, I spotted a black speck in the sky—the E-Group ship. As I drew near, the rear hatch opened and a teenager in black clothing appeared. Before I could react, my vision blurred and everything around me was cold. Deathly cold.

What's going on—?

As I plummeted towards the ground, I understood what had happened. I was surrounded by ice on all sides. The kid who had attacked me had Chad's powers. I focused on expanding the tiny gap between me and the ice, but it was hard to concentrate.

Everything was spinning around me. I would slam into the ground in seconds. Focusing on the tiny space before my eyes, I expanded it and the ice on my face blasted away. Now for the rest!

Kra-ack!

It flew off me like a shell, and not a second

too soon. By now I was only a few hundred feet above ground. My eyes desperately searched for the ship, but it was already gone. I was already over New York City with the UN building only minutes away.

Then I spotted a dot on the horizon. Increasing speed, I had almost caught up with it when a huge metal boulder formed off the stern of the vessel and flew towards me as if propelled from a cannon.

Ebony and Dan did this all the time, but these kids didn't have their experience. The boulder went flying past me.

Which was fine—except I wasn't their target. The boulder was only a diversion. It fell at a terrifying speech towards a housing block below. If it struck, it would kill hundreds of people. I raced after it.

Faster, I thought. *Faster!*

At the last instant, I was able to grab the air around it and divert the rock towards a nearby park.

I needed to disable the vessel, and end this, once and for all. Zooming under the ship, I fired a cannonball of air at it. One of its engines exploded, and it rocked wildly. Good. Now I just needed to drag it downwards and force it to land.

But then a fiery blast emitted from the rear. We were close to Liberty International Airport where numerous planes were in the process of taking off or landing. The blast struck the tail of a passing plane—an A380—hundreds of feet from the ground. The tail exploded into pieces, sending the plane into a dive towards earth. I grabbed the fuselage, but the damage at the back was making it rock wildly. It tore from my grasp. I made a grab for a wing, but only succeeded in making it break loose.

Now the plane was in freefall. I caught a glimpse of a window where a woman was peering out. The expression on her face was of complete terror.

The wing went flying past me, crashing onto an empty tarmac as the plane fell like a rock. Creating a protective bubble around the aircraft, I stabilized it. It was only a hundred feet from the ground. I needed to land this thing—and now!

I was over the northern end of the airport.

Breaking hard to slow the aircraft's forward momentum, I gently brought the aircraft down onto the nearest runway. The remaining wing sheared off, but finally it was motionless on the ground.

Touchdown.

Looking back up, I was just in time to see a plume of smoke rising from the east side of Manhattan.

I was too late.

Chapter Thirty-Six

Crossing the city in seconds, I spotted the E-Group airship on the forecourt of the UN building. A dozen security guards had already been attacked, their bodies bloody and unmoving.

This was going to be a massacre. Flying straight through the windows of the main foyer, I immediately saw another injured security guard on the ground. The foyer spread out ahead—a vast multilayered section with open mezzanine sections stretching all the way to the ceiling.

The E-Group teenagers were dashing across the foyer. They would be in the main assembly hall within seconds.

Zooming low, I created a mini tornado above them. A few tried using their powers against me, but I was too fast. Within seconds I had scooped them up in a vast, whirling column of air. Crushing them into an jumble of arms and legs, I heaped them in the forecourt and sucked the air away, creating a vacuum.

People don't do well when they can't breathe.

It took two minutes for them to all fall

unconscious. By then, dozens of police officers were storming the area. The pilot of the black vessel was placed under arrest. A few officers looked like they wanted to arrest me too, but it's not easy arresting someone fifty feet over your head.

Glancing out onto the road, I saw a figure in a black suit. His face was scarred, but his expression was one of intense loathing. Under other circumstance I wouldn't have recognized him, but I remembered what the others had told me.

Ravana.

He turned and disappeared down an alley. Zooming through the air, I spotted him heading towards a black van. The only thing going through my mind was revenge. The first time we met, he'd tortured me for information. This time, he'd captured my friends with the intention of holding them hostage for the rest of their lives. I was more than happy to see him rot in jail forever.

All this was going through my mind—which was unfortunate, because it meant I didn't see the equipment in the van. I was still ten feet above the ground when the zeno emitter hit me, killing my powers. Hitting the ground hard, I felt something twist in my left foot as I landed, and my head slammed into the pavement.

Within seconds, a mass of arms and legs were on me, dragging me into the van.

'No,' I moaned.

This was history repeating itself. When I had first gained my powers, I had been kidnapped by Ravana. He had unsuccessfully tried to extract information from me. This couldn't be happening to me again. Not again.

But it was.

Dragged into the van, a needle was injected into my arm. The last thing I saw before passing out was Ravana's laughing face.

Opening my eyes next, I found my hands and feet handcuffed to a chair, a zeno emitter directly above. My left foot was aching badly. It wasn't broken, but I wouldn't be running marathons any time soon. Struggling against my metal bonds, I quickly realized there was no way out of this.

My heart was beating furiously. When Ravana returned, he would want to take revenge on me for foiling his plan. Not only had he lost Brodie and the others, but he had lost his opportunity for making us pay for destroying his appearance.

Well, now he would get his chance.

The door eased open and Doctor Ravana and a guard entered. The image went through my mind of him in flames when he had tried to kill us. Would he listen to a mercy plea? I doubted it.

'Ah,' he said. 'We have come full circle. The air boy has come back to me. The last time we met, I asked you questions, but you were unable to give me answers.'

'What do you want to know?' I groaned.

'Nothing!' the man smiled, revealing a line of thin teeth. 'This time there is no need for questions. I want nothing from you. Nothing at all.'

I stared at him.

'Of course,' he continued, 'it is not quite that easy. When I was a young man, women in the street used to turn and look at me. I was a fine specimen. As

I grew older, the women did not look as often, but still I was vain about my appearance.' He frowned. 'I imagine girls look at you. They see your pretty young face and you swell with pride. You dream of a future filled with a wife and family.'

Ravana picked up a scalpel. 'Girls will still look at you when I've finished,' he said. 'But they will look at you as they look at me, with fear, horror and revulsion.' He turned to the guard. 'Boris, the injection.'

The guard picked up a needle.

'This needle will immobilize you,' Ravana said. 'You will be unable to move, or make a sound. But you will feel everything that happens to you.'

Looking into Ravana's eyes, I saw a look of complete hatred.

Boris came close, lifted the needle high...and plunged it into Ravana's arm. The doctor screamed and tried to slash Boris with the scalpel, but was too late. The guard had already stepped out of reach. His features softened, melted and he changed.

'Quinn!' I cried.

'The one and only,' she said.

Ravana had fallen to the floor, his eyes open, but unable to move. Quinn searched his pockets, removed a set of keys and had the handcuffs off me in seconds. I rubbed my wrists.

'How did you find me?'

'My father placed trackers on each of us just in case things went wrong.'

I remembered him grasping my shoulder back at the old lady's house. Normally I would have been furious about being tagged, but I could hardly complain about it. His actions had saved my life.

'Are you alone?' I asked.

'The others are outside. Chad wanted to storm the building—'

'He would.'

'—but I pointed out they might kill you out of revenge,' she finished. 'I convinced them to let me do this alone.'

'Thanks,' I said. 'For everything.'

'We're not out of trouble yet. There's a dozen doors between us and freedom. This place is built from reinforced steel. Even with your powers, it's probably almost impossible to break apart. Trying to get past the guards, a million things could go wrong.' She pointed down at Ravana. 'And then there's him. What do you want to do?'

There were a million things I could say—or do—to this man. He had, after all, tried to destroy us more than once.

Instead, I bent low, peering into his hate-filled eyes. 'I'm sorry about what happened to you,' I said. 'I'm sorry you were badly injured. But you *were* trying to kill us at the time. I could do terrible things to you, but there's already enough hatred in the world. I don't need to make anymore.'

We would inform the authorities about this place. They would come and arrest Ravana and his men. No doubt they would all spend a good many years in jail.

As we started for the door, Quinn gave my hand a quick squeeze. She was right. We would be lucky to get out of here alive.

Good thing I didn't believe in luck.

Chapter Thirty-Seven

'Welcome to my home,' Mr Okada said.

'It's...it's...' I struggled for words. 'It's a missile silo.'

'It is indeed.'

Mr Okada's residence was an old military base, set into the side of a hill in West Virginia. Located in the Monongahela National Forest, the area was dominated by a mountain range covered in red spruce, firs and mountain ash. Sparkling rivers and streams ran through virgin valleys. Eagles flew overhead and deer frolicked in the undergrowth.

A low lying stone building, it was nestled among trees, impossible to see from above, and only visible at eye level if you were standing next to it. The plush interior had windows that overlooked quiet green hills and valleys that stretched into the distance. Not another building was in sight.

Beneath it was an old underground army base, six stories deep, and designed to survive a nuclear attack. The lower sections even had the old equipment in them; computers and control panels from the nineteen fifties.

Circular tunnels, lined with reinforced concrete, linked each section. Three underground missile silos, now empty, were adjacent to a fourth chamber that housed *Liber8tor*. Quinn and I had escaped Doctor Ravana's clutches. He was now residing in a New York City prison, as the result of a tipoff to police.

How he survived being turned to salt was a mystery—and would remain one for the time being.

We were gathered in the plush living room like shags on a rock. It had been so long since we'd had a real place to call home that no-one was quite sure how to behave.

Chad asked the question that was foremost on our minds. 'Is this safe?' he said. 'I mean, the authorities...?'

'I purchased this place several years ago,' Mr Okada said. 'It was legal and above board. The Department of Defense has sold many of these old facilities over the years, now that the cold war is over. I've made some modifications to bring it up to scratch.'

'They're pretty impressive modifications,' Brodie spoke up. 'I had a peek down below. One of the levels is as big as a theater. It looks like it's been set up as a training facility.'

'It has.'

'To train what...exactly?' Ebony said. 'Or should I say, who?'

Mr Okada smiled. 'All in good time.'

'Most of the computers are pretty old,' Dan said. 'But there's a few that are really high tech.' He paused. 'In fact, they're so advanced they look kind of...well...'

'Otherworldly?'

Dan nodded.

'Perhaps it is best if you settle in,' Mr Okada said. 'Rooms have been prepared.'

'Who says we're staying?' Chad asked. 'We've got things to do. People to see Super villains to vanquish.'

'We can stay,' Ebony said, glaring at Chad. 'For a while.'

Our quarters were on the next level down. We each had our own room. Porthole windows had been carved into the rock, allowing in light and a glimpse of the outside world. My room was warm and comfortable, fitted out with a television, computer and a games console. I glanced at the games.

If all the rooms are like this, I thought, *Dan will be in Heaven.*

Brodie appeared in the doorway.

'Hey,' she said. 'Thoughts?'

'Oh,' I said, airily, 'it's all right.'

We laughed. This was the lap of luxury compared to the quarters on *Liber8tor*.

'How are you feeling?' I asked. 'It's not every day that your brain gets taken over by a computer.'

As we sat down on my bed, I was suddenly aware that this was the closest we'd been in a long time. A barrier had formed between us when we had journeyed to the future—and a lot of it had been of my own making. Sometimes walls made of anger are more difficult to overcome than those made of stone or steel. For the first time since then, I wondered if there could be a new beginning between us.

'The back of my head is still sore,' Brodie said. 'But I feel surprisingly okay, considering what we went through.' She frowned at me. 'More's the question, how do you feel? You gained your family, only to lose them again.'

I nodded. It was taking time to process my feelings.

'I was taken in completely,' I admitted. 'I believed what they said about my parents. I believed Quinn was my ex-girlfriend. I believed Louise and Henry were my aunt and uncle. The longer I stayed, the more real it became. But you know the worst part?'

'What?'

'I *wanted* to believe it was real.'

'There's nothing wrong in that,' Brodie said, taking my hand. 'Family is important.'

I gave her hand a squeeze. 'I've got everything I need right here,' I said. 'Well, almost everything.'

We looked into each other's eyes.

'I've missed you,' Brodie said.

'I've missed you, too.'

As I leant towards her, a sound came from the door.

'Sorry,' Quinn said. 'I didn't mean to interrupt.'

'That's okay,' I said, letting go of Brodie's hand. 'What is it?'

'Dad wants us in the living room.'

We met the others in the corridor. As we climbed the stairs, I thought about each of them— Brodie, Chad, Dan, Ebony and Ferdy. Maybe they were all the family I'd ever need.

Mr Okada directed us to plush chairs in the living room. 'Please take a seat,' he said. 'Would anyone like a drink?'

'Sure,' Chad said, 'as long as it's not lemonade.'

As Mr Okada went to fetch refreshments, Quinn plonked herself onto a couch opposite me. So much had happened over the last few days that I felt like I'd known her for years. She didn't look like

Brodie now. She looked like herself.

I wouldn't want her any other way.

As she gave me a small smile, I glanced over at Brodie. She was staring at me with a troubled expression. *Don't tell me she's jealous.* That was the last thing I needed. Giving me a sad smile, she jumped up and helped Mr Okada with glasses and bottles of soft drink.

'You must have a lot of questions,' he said, after drinks were served.

'Only one or two hundred,' I said. 'People usually don't do very well after they've had a bullet to the brain.'

Mr Okada nodded. 'All right,' he said. 'That's a good start.' Taking a sip of coke, he said, 'My name is Robert Okada. At least, that's the name I've used for many years. You would not be able to pronounce my real name.'

'Why?'

'Because I am an alien,' he said. 'I am Bakari.'

Bakari? The Bakari were an alien race that

had lived on Earth for thousands of years. They had been behind the Alpha Project, working with The Agency to create superheroes. We were the result of one of those experiments.

We had already met two of the Bakari, but this guy was nothing like them. Those Bakari named themselves after numbers—Twelve and Twenty-Two—and were Caucasian. Mr Okada was Japanese—or appeared to be.

'How old are you?' Brodie asked Mr Okada.

'Nine thousand years. Give or take a few centuries.'

He looked good for his age.

'We were told the Bakari had all left Earth,' Ebony said.

'They have,' Mr Okada said, nodding. 'I am the last Bakari, but I have not been aligned with my people for some time.'

'Why?'

'We had differences of opinion. I was opposed to the superhero program. I felt it was immoral to destroy a person's past, and make them face an uncertain future.'

'No arguments there,' Chad said.

'Why did they leave?' I asked.

'A great war is being waged. It began with the Tagaar's aborted invasion of Earth. When their attempt failed, the Union of Planets—'

'Who are they?' Dan interrupted. 'I forget.'

'The Union is an intergalactic league that makes the laws that govern the civilized worlds. They are very much like the United Nations. When Earth was attacked, the Union demanded that Tagaar withdraw from other disputed territories it had held for the last year. When they refused, the Union declared war.'

'War,' Ebony echoed.

'Interstellar war,' Mr Okada confirmed. 'At this moment, a hundred species are fighting thousands of battles against the Tagaar across the length and breadth of the galaxy.'

'Surely the Union will win,' I said.

'The Tagaar are a warrior race. They would prefer to die than be defeated. Ancient Tagaar texts state that they must constantly grow their territory, or they will die out.'

'What will happen?' Chad asked.

'They will fight to the death.'

'This all sounds really...chilling,' Brodie said. 'Apocalyptic, actually. But what's it got to do with us?'

'Ultimately, that war will come to Earth,' Mr Okada said. 'And the results will be devastating when it does. Earth is in no condition to defend itself. There can only be one outcome when the Tagaar return— the complete destruction of your world.'

Dead silence filled the room.

'I hope it doesn't happen before the next Star Wars movie comes out,' Chad said. 'I've been dying to see it.'

'Chad...' Brodie groaned, rolling her eyes.

Mr Okada smiled gently. 'It is common to make jokes when faced with a grave situation,' he said. 'I know humans quite well, having lived among you for so long. It tears my heart apart to know that you are doomed.'

'It doesn't exactly thrill me either,' Chad said.

'You sound pretty resigned,' I said to Mr Okada. 'If you know us so well, you also know we don't give up. We'll do everything we can to defend ourselves.'

'I know. And you will fail. Earth is not equipped to defeat an alien race as technologically advanced as the Tagaar. It will be like an ant trying to defeat a man with a flamethrower.'

'I've got an off-topic question,' Chad intervened. 'How can Quinn be your daughter? Or is she an alien too?'

'She is my daughter. The Bakari experience love just as other races.'

'I'm half-human,' Quinn explained, 'and half-Bakari. I am transform myself into anyone providing we're roughly the same size.'

To prove her point, she turned herself into a complete copy of Chad.

'That's creepy,' I said. 'One Chad is bad enough.'

She transformed back.

'So what are we doing here?' Chad asked. 'We appreciate the comfy chairs and all, but...'

'I hope you will make this your home,' Mr Okada said. 'You can train here, hone your skills and learn the true extend of your powers.'

'And then?' I asked.

'And then you will be ready for whatever happens.'

None of us said anything for what seemed an eternity. Then Dan spoke up.

'I vote, yes,' he said.

Ebony nodded. 'Me too,' she said. 'I don't mind staying for a while.'

'Ferdy votes yes, too,' Ferdy's voice came through the intercom.

'You can hear us?' I said.

'Ferdy is patched into the Asgard communications array.'

'Argard?'

'The name of this military base,' Ferdy said. 'Named after one of the nine worlds in Norse mythology, it—'

'Thanks, Ferdy,' I interrupted. 'Brodie?'

'Gotta sleep somewhere,' she said, shrugging. 'Might as well be here.'

Chad's eyes settled on me. 'Looks like it's up to you and me,' he said.

'And?'

'Yes,' he said. 'The beds here are better than *Liber8tor*. The food's got to be an improvement and we need a place to call home.'

Home.

'But it needs to be unanimous,' he added.

I swallowed. Maybe we would never find our parents. Maybe we would never discover our true identities. Maybe we would be forever searching. The answers to life weren't always straightforward. Mostly they were messy and incomplete. The world had a way of taking you places you didn't expect, and dishing out pain you didn't deserve.

But everyone needed a place to call home. A place to prepare for whatever the future had in store.

Even a bunch of teenage superheroes.

'All right,' I said. 'I vote—yes.'

A Few Final Words

I hope you enjoyed reading Terminal Fear. The other books in the Teen Superheroes series are:

Diary of a Teenage Superhero (Book One)

The Doomsday Device (Book Two)

The Battle for Earth (Book Three)

The Twisted Future (Book Four)

Thanks again and happy reading!

Darrell